A
Truth
In
Ruby

Jessica Florence

Jessica Florence© 2020

Editing by Magnifico Manuscripts

Proofreading by Virginia Tesi Carey

Cover by Sarah Hansen, Okay Creations ©

Chapter One

Sapphira

"Princess Sapphira, I remember you now."

The goat Fae's shocked face made me laugh. My mother's power over Emrys and everyone else's mind in the kingdom was tied to the onyx tomb. Now that it had been opened, everyone remembered my true identity.

Tears rolled down Dris's shimmering cheeks, and I wanted to hug her and thank her for helping me. From that very first day in the library, the owl Fae had stood by my side. Now we needed to come up with a detailed plan on how I'd fulfill my vow to return magic to the realm.

"It's been you the whole time." The rage in Rune's shocked voice struck me like a bullet in my heart.

My knees wobbled from the sight of my mate. As expected, sorrow and guilt hit me when I met his silent fury-filled stare. I had so much to discuss with him, including the relationship with his brother, Tor, on our travels here. Instantly, I felt weary from all the conversations to come and squared my shoulders to face the consequences.

"Do you remember everything?" Tor asked, feeling the tension rising between his brother and me.

"I remember everything from my time as a human, everything before that is spotty." I diverted my gaze to the others. Desmire, my father, sat calmly next to the melted tomb, and my mother stood in front of him. Her graceful hand rested on his side while my parents looked at me.

The memories she gave me of a human childhood with Mariam were still in my head. When I was a human, I didn't have parents besides Mariam, and now as a Fae I did. They loved me so much, they wrecked their lives to save mine.

Rune stomped out of the room, and my throat constricted. I wanted to run after him, to explain, to beg for his forgiveness.

"What do we do now?" Dris asked.

I blinked my tears away. "We station more guards at the realm ports of entry. Now that we've exposed ourselves, and where we are generally located, the Dramens will search without rest for us." Besides Tor, no one else had suffered at the Dramens's violent human hands yet.

"Soon, I will be traveling to Crystoria to find out where the legendary Heart Tree is. It must be restored from its sickened state and then if my plan works the way it should, magic will be free once again, hopefully, before Verin or the Dramens start a war." I prayed to the universe that I could do this, or the last twenty years were for nothing.

My magic pulsed in my chest, giving me the hope to ignore the doubts. After everything I'd gone through to get here, the human Sapphira and the Fae Princess were merged. I was both. Where the weaknesses of the human version failed, the Fae version took over, and vice versa.

"I'll be with you on this journey." Emrys smiled broadly, accepting who I was and still happily bound to me as a spy via a blood oath.

"Me too!" Dris excitedly raised her hand. I wasn't sure if she was more elated as a librarian going to Crystoria with their great library or as a best friend uncovering the mystery before us.

"As will I." Tor smiled his sweet grin . . . always the protector.

"Great. We have lots to do and not a lot of time to do it." I gave them my best smile, hoping it showed them I was confident in myself and this plan.

"Moon," my mother whispered and I walked toward her. I remembered her and we were a family again. Father looked into my eyes and I wished he wasn't stuck as a dragon so I could hear his voice, feel his big arms around me.

"Mother." I touched her pale cheek softly. Tears rolled down her cheeks as she embraced me, her hands trembling against my back.

"I love you, Mother. Thank you for everything." I didn't know if she understood me since she went crazy after expending all her powers to change the memories of the kingdom. Still, I surrounded her with warmth and love.

"Moon, moon, moon," she sang, and pulled back. Her smile sparkled, and she lightly pushed me away. She was telling me to go. There was so much to do, so much I needed to figure out.

"Princess?" Tor stepped away from Dris and Emrys, who were talking to Nyx, my oldest friend and handmaiden. Tor's energy crashed into me. I needed to say something, anything to show him where I stood.

"I do love you. That will never change, but I know what you are to Rune, and I know I can't compete." Nothing in his posture declared he was upset about his words.

"Why did you even start anything with me if you knew?"

"I didn't know for sure. I just remembered what the princess looked like in my dreams, and Nyx was not it. I sort of put it together why the seer Celestine told me to find you. I think a part of me thought that you being away from Rune, without your memory . . . that your heart might fall for me. But another part of me knew it wasn't going to happen, even when you said you loved me. I knew you meant it but not like the love you have for him."

My chest ached for him. A defeated look began to show in his deep blue eyes.

"I want to assist you in this journey. I need to do this." He clenched his fist.

"Of course you're coming with us. You have always been my protector." I hugged him and sighed, grateful that Tor hadn't given into my demands to sleep with him before I regained my memory. Otherwise the guilt would have eaten me alive. I would have hated him and myself.

"I think he's going to need some serious groveling." Tor pulled back from my embrace and gave me his smile that I loved.

"Heart Tree help me."

"You might need more than a legendary tree to help face a pissed-off werewolf."

"Thank you for finding me and bringing me here." I leaned over to kiss his cheek then walked toward the exit. I had a mate to find and beg for forgiveness.

Chapter Two

Rune

Twenty years.

I'd thought my mate was trapped in onyx for twenty years. Meanwhile, she lived in the dangerous human world as one of them.

The Dramens had touched her. She had been alone, and then Tor . . . I wanted to kill him. He'd had her, my mate, the other half of my being. She had loved him and was willing to sacrifice everything to save him.

"Fuck!" I roared into the legendary Hallowstag Woods. I needed to go somewhere quiet and away from any casualties of my rage.

She had lied to me. She kept her plan hidden from me, and I stayed here waiting like a god damn puppy for her instead of scouring the earth to find her. Rage flooded my vision and I punched a dead tree until blood ran from my knuckles. Wood splinted into my skin, and the bite barely soothed the internal pain consuming me.

I heard her steps before she entered the clearing.

"I'm sorry." I'd spent almost every night since she arrived thinking of her voice . . . how much I hated it and hated the unwanted warmth it stirred in my stomach.

"Twenty fucking years." I scoffed; her apology wasn't enough.

"Rune." My hands stopped pummeling the wood when my name fell from her lips. A demanding force inside me urged that I go to her, to be with my mate.

"For twenty years I thought you were inside that tomb. I tried everything I could to break it, to get you out of it. I never gave up hope of seeing you again." I faced her. Memories of our past flew through my mind and I shut them down. I'd been tricked, made to believe I loved someone else.

"I tried everything, and in reality, you were out in the human world. Completely at the hands of survivors, and those cruel bastards. Meanwhile, I was here pining over a woman who wasn't mine." The wolf within roared, my hands ripping the broken section of tree. I threw it as far as I could.

"Rune, I did what I had to. Verin wanted magic gone and it was the only way I could save everyone. I didn't do it to spite you. I became a human and went through it all to save you." She took a confident step closer, the only person on the damn planet that would approach me with such ease while I was pissed. She'd never been afraid of me.

"I'd do it again, if given the choice. I took a wild gamble to protect my kingdom and the people I love most. I was willing to become human for our people to have a fighting chance in the future. We would have been ruined if I had stayed." She took one last step, and I trembled from the heat of her body caressing me.

"You done?" I snarled and watched her face pinch with regret.

"We could have figured it out. Together. Instead you plotted without me and you suffered while I pined for that pretender in onyx. I failed as a mate to protect you. Those dirty creatures touched you, violated you while I talked to a sleeping woman about what we'd do when she got out."

She reached out with tears brimming her eyes to touch my face. I shifted away. Betrayal stung and I needed space.

"Fine, you need your time. I can see it. But know this. I lost all my memories when I took out my core, and even without knowing you existed, I felt the mating bond the whole time. Somewhere out there this unyielding force waited for me, called to me. I'm sorry for the pain I caused you, but I won't regret doing what I did. Now I'm gonna save us all again and carry the weight of my choices as I go." She quickly turned, and my hurt slipped through the crack of my lips.

"Despite whatever you felt, you still left me, and fell in love with Tor." It was a poisoned barb but my anger was too far gone to take it back.

She didn't stop walking or face me. I was too pissed to play nice, and she needed to think about her next steps. In that onyx room she'd mentioned she didn't remember everything. Depending on the memories she saw clearly, her attachment to me could be less than hers to Tor.

I stomped off, wishing I could shed my skin and become the beast, who rattled within, wanting to reunite with its mate. Guilt ate me from the inside with every gaze I'd let linger on Sapphira, every time I wished to kiss her while she looked like the answer to a prayer I should have asked for. All the signs were there, and I'd been too stubborn to listen to what my core tried to tell me. I knew Sapphira was mine, down to her very essence, even before I knew I had the right to claim her. I looked at the early morning sky, ready for moonlight to come and set me free of these thoughts for one more night. With heavy steps I walked farther into the Hallowstags . . . and my pain.

Chapter Three

Sapphira

His words stung like the slice of a blade in my heart. I walked through the city of Crysia as people began their morning routines. I feared their recognition of me, and the fallout from our deception. We needed to make a statement soon, but not while I meandered the cobblestone paths toward the palace. My perception of this Fae realm had changed once I resumed being Princess Sapphira.

Well . . . not completely. I couldn't remember everything. I remembered my mother as a strong and fierce ruler, which her diamond core gave her. I remembered my father as the strongest Fae male in the land with his dragon and onyx essence.

I made it to the palace and meandered through the stone hallways to the room that housed me before my memories returned. Conflict chewed at my thoughts. I know this room wasn't mine anymore. Princesses don't sleep in servants' quarters, but it was still home.

I opened the door and walked to sit on the one-person bed.

"I had a feeling I'd find you here." Nyx smiled at me.

"It feels weird going anywhere else," I admitted, and she plopped down beside me.

"I was in the onyx for twenty years pretending to be you, but it feels like it was only yesterday I laid on that altar. I didn't experience anything new, and my memories aren't muddled." She rested her head against my shoulder, and I reached for her hand. Being a survivor of the apocalypse had left me constantly craving touch from other humans.

"It's a mess in my head."

"Well, you've always been off in the head," she teased and I laughed. Nyx "got" me, and I had missed that.

"Thank you for—"

"I am honored to have done my duty, but it's not over, my princess."

She was right. The overwhelming destiny ahead of me seemed impossible: figure out where the Heart Tree rested; return magic; fight in a potential war with the Dramens; deal with Verin; win my mate back; and return to princess duties and training.

"Fuck." I groaned, wishing I had fifteen of me right now.

"You have people behind you, Sapphira. You are not alone." Her powers emanating from her amethyst core, comforting me.

Changing the subject, she asked, "How did it go with Rune?"

"He's pissed, and rightfully so. The warrior is stubborn. I had hoped he would be happy that the princess in the tomb and the human he was drawn to were actually one person, but he feels betrayed."

I longed to run into his arms and feel his strength and love.

"He'll come around. He's just being normal, grumpy-ass Rune." Nyx squeezed my hand and I took a deep breath. Nyx had never feared my mate. She had helped me sneak around to see him and kept my secrets when I was technically engaged to his brother.

"I hope so."

"Girl, you don't need hope. That wolf pined over you for twenty years and never gave up. He never let anyone else in until you landed in his lap as a human. And you were really his mate the whole time, so the only other person he cared for was you both times. Human or Fae princess, he loved you either way."

My lavender-haired friend knew what to say to lift my spirits. I needed to keep the faith of our bond burning within me.

"Thanks, Nyx." She hugged me then stood, her hand still holding mine.

"You're welcome." She pulled me up slowly, and I stood, begrudgingly.

"Unfortunately, now that you are the princess again, we have to get you back into the swing of things.

First step is getting your room ready and you clean. You'll be expected to speak tonight in the throne room."

I just wanted to sleep and did not want to go back to that terrifying tomb of a room. I sighed again and left the room I'd lived in for the last month. No one bothered us on our way up to the royal wing. The rooms on this floor of the palace were lavishly decorated in carpets, art, and metal, unlike the stone walls where servants stayed.

"Gross." Nyx looked around, and I shared her sentiment.

The room was covered in cobwebs and dust. When I had vanished from the realm and Nyx laid in the onyx, my mother had closed the door to my suite and never opened it.

"This is not a room for a princess." She waved her hand in the air, and I felt the essence within her spread throughout the room.

The dust seeped away, and the cobwebs disappeared. Seconds passed, and my room slowly turned into the beautiful suite it was before years of solitude had taken over.

"We'll still have to get new dresses and bedding, but at least everything else is clean." Thanks to her amethyst core, she had purified my room.

"Thank you." I felt like I was forever thanking her for taking care of me, but she waved me off and ripped the comforter off my bed. "Don't you want to rest?"

"What I want is to be by your side and make sure you keep being the badass princess I know you are. No buts." She shushed me before I could retort. I perched my behind onto the seat by the vanity.

"It's my purpose, Sapphira, and I enjoy this. I want to be here." She looked at me sweetly and I nodded. My own emotions were a wreck and it wasn't fair to push them onto her. I needed to deal with myself.

"Now I'll start the bath and rally a dress for tonight. If you can't make people see your side of things, then we will distract them with that killer body of yours."

Minutes later, I sank into my large marble bath, soaking the soreness out of my muscles from the weight of my burdens.

Chapter Four

Sapphira

I stared at the hairbrush on the vanity while Drys and Nyx played with my hair like I was a child's doll. I didn't remember using the brush. I didn't remember a lot of my memories with Rune. Having amnesia sucked. I had a few little glimpses into my past via Celestine's dreams, like the time Rune slipped on a mossy rock by the waterfall and I laughed before jumping into the crisp water with him, kissing his wet, grumpy lips. I saw memories of how we fought the bond between us while Tor attempted to woo me. I smiled with a memory of his werewolf form nuzzling my neck and holding me. We'd walk in the Hallowstag Woods together, living in nature until the full moon shifted. But that was it. I had memories of Tor, both human and some Fae. I'd always loved him, but not like I loved Rune when I was Princess Sapphira.

Love.

I knew Rune was my mate, and I felt some of the love I had for him in our past, but I wasn't sure I was there in the present. I cared deeply for him and wanted to be with him, but it didn't have the chance to grow into that love I'd dreamed of before I'd been thrust back in Fae form. I craved the love we'd shared twenty years ago. But fear continued to haunt me that we didn't love each other like we did before because we were different now.

Where did that leave us?

"You need to fix that face, Princess." Nyx placed a sapphire-jeweled comb in the braids she'd twisted alongside my head.

I looked like a Viking princess I had seen on an old movie case years ago as a human, and the black shadow around my eyes accentuated the look of warrior princess. Both of my friends thought I needed to look the part—savior of the land—so people wouldn't challenge me tonight.

"It's going to be OK. Everyone will understand that you and your mother did what you did to save us. You have magic, a powerful magic that can return us back to our natural state with nature and defeat Verin. If you hadn't devised your plan, you'd be stuck like us. We'd still be under Verin's thumb." Dris stared into my soul with her all-seeing, owl-like eyes.

I was glad she didn't care that I was the princess. To her I was no different than Sapphira the human.

Don't get me wrong I could easily appreciate the perks of being a princess who had everything she could ever want hand delivered to her. But now I see why I used to seek out adventure in the Hallowstags. When Tor and I travelled across the continent together, searching for this place I dreamed of relaxing at the human safe haven for the remainder of my years. Then everything changed. I changed. I didn't even know who I was anymore.

"At least you'll be able to handle the wine better in your Fae body," Dris snickered, and Nyx looked back and forth between us, clearly missing the tease. Dris explained how trashed I had gotten the last time I had attended a ball before being kidnapped by Verin's men.

"Oh I would have loved to see that. You never drank a lot before. You liked to keep your head clear." Nyx chuckled and lightly ran her fingers over my hair, flecks of purple stones shimmered over my hair like amethyst dust. I reached up to clasp her hand and squeeze it. She missed a lot lying in the tomb for twenty years, and while I know to her it felt like the blink of an eye, I knew she would have troubles adapting to all the changes.

"All right, let's get you in that dress and get you down to greet your people." Dris carried over a wispy dress that had lots of straps. Somehow, we managed to get the dress on me without breaking a sweat, and as I looked in the mirror, I grimaced. The Fae were sensual beings, and I'd seen way more provocative dresses in the last month but never on me.

A vibrant turquoise material covered my breasts, then branched out like vines connecting to the chiffon blue skirt that flared into a red coloring all the way to the floor. The dress reminded me of a sunset, which would normally be soothing but with all the skin showing except for the material covering my breasts, ass, and sex, the dress told the tale of a confident woman of power, a princess who would one day rule all of Crysia like her mother.

"Wow. You look hot!" Dris's eyes somehow widened.

I felt strong and somewhat like my old self. Even now in my weighted mindset, I knew I could play the part I needed. Dris was already dressed in a flowing cream gown with shimmering sleeves that came to a point over the top of her hand. It had a see-through back, and her hair was wild as smoke. She'd be my escort while Nyx finished dressing herself, claiming she needed extra time to get ready for her first big reveal in twenty years. Although she liked serving as my handmaiden, she also loved the glam of our life. Nyx loved to dress up in fashions of her own designs. She didn't do it for the attention of the males in our city, she did it for herself which made me love her even more.

My owl friend walked with me down the familiar halls to the ball, music echoing throughout the palace, and I remembered how much I had wished to dance at them while I sat in my servant's quarters as a human.

Thoughts of Rune dressed up for the evening and holding me close while we danced crossed my mind. However, he still had one night left in his werewolf form. At least Tor would be there, a constant comfort beside me, even as a human. Conflicting emotions roiled in my gut when I thought of our time as a couple.

"Fuck, my life is a mess," I admitted out loud, wanting nothing more than to go back to my room and work on sorting my shit out.

"Yeah, it is, but we'll clean it up, one dirty section at a time." Dris's sympathetic smile didn't ease my stress, but her words balmed the ache in my head a little bit.

Just as we were about to reach the room where I'd have to face my first challenge, a loud howl echoed outside the palace. The moon held my mate prisoner for one more night. Maybe, the beast craved to be close to me like I was for him.

Chapter Five

Sapphira

"I knew it was you the whole time."

"We are so glad you're back, now we can have someone on the throne that isn't crazy."

"You look a little rough, dear. I can't believe you were in the human world for all these years. Very disappointing."

I now remembered how much I disliked the Fae elites at these gatherings. They were snobby, and only like to show off while working for their best interests. Men flocked to me, hoping I'd make them my king, saying I was the most beautiful princess in the land, and I deserved a man who would keep me pretty while dealing with ruling the kingdom himself.

My mother swayed to the music and her advisor Ryka was at her side. I let mother enjoy the party. It warmed my heart that despite her losing her mind while altering everyone else's, she never gave up her cheerful essence.

"You look like you're ready to bury someone in the queen's gardens." Tor's voice broke through my thoughts.

"I can't say I missed being the center of attention at these gatherings."

Tor had cut his brown messy hair and cleaned up the stubble growing on his jaw. He looked nice in a fancy tunic, pants, and knee-high boots—like the prince of many princesses's dreams.

"I almost didn't recognize you dressed like a fancy prince." Tor offered his hand for me to dance with him. I accepted, needing space from everyone else vying for my attention. Tor was safe, and he always knew when I fell deep into my thoughts.

"I didn't recognize you, although, I remember you before your human years now. You look the same except for the weighted expression in your eyes." I looked into his soulful brown eyes and the tension eased within.

"I don't feel like I know who I am anymore." I whispered low enough for only Tor to hear, and not the other Fae.

"You're still you. Same spunky spirit, smart-ass mouth, gorgeous body, and a big destiny that you always had."

"You always make me laugh."

"What can I say. I'm a funny guy, and I'm glad that hasn't changed. Although, I'd thought with you being a fancy princess, you would have access to a big bath. You're still making my eyes water." He grinned, and I smacked his shoulder lightly. I knew he was trying to make me forget about everything and enjoy the ball.

"I knew you'd be a good dancer." I thought about all the times I imagined him dancing while I worked in the palace.

"I'm good at everything." He waggled his eyebrows suggestively, and I shook my head. A month ago, I would have tackled him to the floor and ripped his clothes off, screaming for him to prove his words. Now, remorse and shame flooded my thoughts. I wronged him and that hurt my heart.

"I think I've had enough for tonight. These spoiled Fae don't really care about what I did. They stayed rich and got what they wanted over the twenty years. Tomorrow, I'll go out to the city. They are the people that I need to grovel to." I released my grip on his shoulder, and he took a step back.

"I still love you, Sapphira, no matter what." He gave me a grim smile before walking off. I watched his retreated form.

"Time to go?" Nyx sauntered to my side and I nodded.

"Please stay, though. You have lost time to make up for and I bet some pent-up energy." I prayed she took the free time I offered, and I wanted to be alone. She eyed me, searching for the real reason I wanted her to stay.

"I just want some alone time, and I know you'll be by my side when the world falls out from under me. So I want you to have fun while you can." I told her the truth and she understood.

"Go rest, Princess." She pulled me into a hug, and I instantly felt calmer. Sometimes when the stress of my birthright became too much, she'd push a bit of her soothing power into me to help me fall asleep easier.

We separated and I strode over to say goodbye to Dris and Emrys, who were sipping wine without muttering a word to each other. Sooner or later, I suspected they would become close friends, given our little circle. However, until then, I enjoyed their back and forth tension.

Finally, I walked up to my mother and gave her a hug. She hugged me back and a sweet song from my childhood melodically flowed past her pink lips. Her brown hair was curled into a bun and her diamond crown twinkled in the torch lights.

"I'm going to bed. I love you."

Even when I was human, I felt a strange pull to the queen. I wanted her happy, and I wanted her approval. My soul recognized who she was before I knew it, and love beamed at my center.

"Moon, moon, moon. Bright and round, searching for a queen who can't be found." She switched from humming my old nursery song to a mixture of words. Maybe a riddle? She had spoken truth in our previous conversations, only I hadn't known to piece them together.

"Thank you." I bowed, taking in her words to analyze later and she smiled.

The walk to my quarters was not as quiet as I'd hoped. Two guards followed me, and while their mouths were shut, the rustling of their weapons against their armor provided an annoying atmosphere. I slammed my door once inside; the frustration had risen past my control.

I looked around the room, and I found no comfort inside. Memories came and went of times spent in this room wearing fancy dresses in all colors and materials, reading books, and drawing from my window seat. While I remembered ease and freedom in this room, I also remembered memories of insanity. When I'd pieced together the mystery between Verin and King Lachan being the same person, I'd gone mad. He knew I was his niece, not his daughter, but no one else knew except my mother. With my power of absorption and time, I would grow to be stronger than he ever could be. With my mother and real father at my side, he would be ruined.

I had locked myself in this gilded cage and obsessed over how to beat him. Hours passed without sleep, and I'd torn through every book, every scroll until I found Debaru's experiments of removing a Fae's essence. I knew my father's power could protect it, but as long as Verin knew I was alive, I'd never be able to grow into my full powers. That's when Nyx and I came up with the plan to place her in onyx with my core while my mother altered everyone's mind to believe she was me.

My gaze shifted toward my wardrobe where I'd scribbled my insanity onto the back of it. I traded my scandalous dress for a short nightgown, then removed my makeup, and released my hair from the braids. Sleep has always been King Verin in disguise, and twenty years ago, he released a sickness upon our world that leaked to the human realm. Half of humanity died, and in our own realm, you—our people—were left stripped of your essence powers. He planned to take away our powers and I did not have the strength to stop him. The only thing I could do was buy us all time. I removed my essence and placed it in the hands of my most honored friend, who rested in an onyx tomb for twenty years, keeping it safe.

"I've spent all that time living as a human in the tragic and dangerous world that was left after Verin's treachery. Now I have returned, ready to serve you, my people, and do everything I can to make our world right again." I fell to my knees and bowed.

"I will hear any grievances now." I rose to my feet and looked them all in the eyes. At first I thought maybe no one would come forward. That maybe they understood why I did what I did and forgave the deceit.

Until the first person came forward, then another, and another.

Chapter Seven

Tor

"How long has she been doing this?" I glanced at Sapphira's purple handmaiden Nyx before watching Sapphira, who was training with Najen, Rune's second-in-command.

"Ever since we got back from talking with the people. Some were nice and understood everything she did and why. Then there were a few who said things I'd rather not repeat." Nyx rubbed her hands against her flowing green dress.

I hated for Sapphira to suffer. "We'll help her through it."

"You know part of her frustrations stem from you, too. You muddled her heart as a human, and those memories are fresher than the Fae ones." Nyx glared at me. She and I were never friends in the past. She thought me to be a flirt. To me, she always acted like a stuck-up Fae bitch. She loved dressing the princess up in fancy clothes and living the life of luxury.

"I'm not going to regret being with her. She's made her choice, and I will be by her side as her friend like I always have. And if my grump of a brother doesn't get his head out of his ass, then I will be waiting with open arms for her, if that's what she wants." I didn't bother looking at have the whole world to choose from. Focus on someone else that isn't a mate with your brother."

I growled at the annoying, self-righteous woman beside me. "Have I done anything at all since she rescued me to show that I am trying to win her heart? I haven't done a damn thing since I've been back but be a supportive friend. What phoenix flew up your ass and burned your attitude? Fuck, what else am I supposed to do, oh one who knows everything? Tie them to the bed together until they make up? I feel like they both might kill me for it, but if it gets you off my back, then fine!"

Nyx turned white and became as silent and still as a statue.

"I am trying hard. I don't remember everything, you jackass!" Sapphira yelled at Rune and threw her sword at him.

"You won't last a day in the coming war. Now pick up that sword and do it again." Rune bared his pointed Fae canines and came at her with blinding speed. She grabbed the sword on the ground and blocked him just in time.

I glanced toward the purple-haired woman beside me and decided it was time to go. I needed to fight someone and release the guilt and anger battling inside me. The handmaiden watched me carefully, her eyes narrowing. She probably believed the fun, flirty, and easygoing Prince Torin would be on to the next beautiful woman in seconds without any emotions.

"Let me know if she needs me." A few pity-filled eyes glanced my way as I departed. Great, now the gossip mill would spread all the details of my outburst. This day was not my day.

Chapter Eight

Sapphira

"Just rub this on the cut and you'll be good as new in a few hours." Rista, the lead healer, handed me a salve to assist my speedy Fae healing to close the slice in my arm quicker. I looked over the wooden container and sniffed the contents. All of the Fae's senses were heightened, and I was still getting used to everything again. It was like I forgot how to be a Fae after living like a human for so long.

"Thanks for patching me up again." I grimaced as the wound on my shoulder shot pain up and down my arm.

"That's what I'm here for." She smiled as I walked out of her healer's hut for a bath and then to meet Dris in the library. We had studying to do. Nyx was quick to join my side as I entered the stone and wooden halls and remained silent as we walked up the stairs to my room.

"I heard Tor yell at you earlier. Is he OK?" I nodded to the guards at the end of the hall and I reached my door.

"I might have antagonized him a bit, but honestly he needs to move on. It's sad watching him pine after you like he does." Nyx headed straight for the bath that I desperately needed. I, however, stopped moving.

"What did you say? Tell me everything!" I loved Nyx, but she had issues with Tor that I never understood. She finished pouring some oils in the bath, then stood in the doorway. My head ached with every word as she explained what had happened.

"I appreciate what you were trying to do, but right now, Nyx, I don't need a champion. I'll figure out my love life on my own. And as much as I want to sort it all this second, I've got bigger things on my shoulders. War with the Dramens, war with Verin, and hopefully finding a damn cure to the sickness he poured into the realms." I stomped to the bath and disrobed quickly. Water touched the cut on my right arm, burning like someone had poured lava on it. I cursed and Nyx was there with an antiseptic oil for me to rub it with.

"I'm sorry. I didn't mean to cause you more stress." Nyx sat next to the tub and gently released her calming powers into the hot water with the swirl of her finger. I needed extra help to soothe everything from my muscles to my mind.

"I just need the people closest to me to get along. One less thing I have to worry about." I closed my eyes and sank under the water. The world disappeared, and I focused again. I felt shame and anger from talking with my people earlier.

"You abandoned us. You'll do it again."

"You and your mother betrayed our trust. We won't stand for this kind of manipulation."

The angry voices echoed in my head and drowned out those who understood and spoke with kindness. Then Rune had to show up to my session with Najen and once again showed me how shitty of a fighter I was. He raged at me, and I wished we could talk about it. However, he turned back into asshole Rune who loved making my training a living hell. He taught me a new move then showed me how to turn a defensive play into an offensive one. I tried the move and ended up slicing my arm with my own sword. Embarrassed and in pain, I immediately stomped toward Rista's hut. Rune didn't chase after me which made my sour mood rot further.

I breathed deeply once my head rose from the water. I'd hoped to relax and enjoy the quietness in the room, but the chatter in my head wasn't done with me.

"I need to get out of here." Panic overcame me, and I needed to be free of these walls, even for a moment.

Nyx covered me with a towel, and I quickly scrubbed my body clean and dried off. I dressed in a long-sleeved tunic, tight pants, and boots, and I did what I used to do in my youth—climbed out the large window of my room. There were never guards in the gardens below, and no one would see as I hoisted myself up the wooden ledge toward the point of the palace roof. My fingers dug into the wood and stone as the wind hit me from the east. My wounded arm throbbed with every flex of my muscles to reach the next delicately carved arched beam. Fae with essences of the earth used their powers to become architects and thousands of years later, it still stood strong.

I jumped over a banister and smiled. There was a small section of space between the large peaks of the palace that I used to get away. It was shaded from the setting sun, and no one would find me here. Only two people knew I hid up here when the palace life became too excessive for me—my mother and Nyx. Both had their own little hideouts around the palace as well, so they never bothered me in mine.

A small box sat hidden in the shadows. I'd left this box here twenty years ago for when I returned. I remember putting important items to me in here but couldn't remember what those items were. I hadn't locked the box, since no one ever came up here but me. However, the seal had damage from the passing years and weather. I pried and dug with my fingernails to open the box but it wouldn't budge.

"Great. Another thing giving me a hard time in my life." I growled and set the box down. I'd really hoped to have one thing go easy for me but that appeared to be a hard request. I sat on the roof of the palace in my hiding spot until the sun set and the moon rose over the mountains surrounding our city. Once the night coated the palace, I snuck down the side facing the woods and made a run for it.

Chapter Nine

Nyx

I sighed as I shaded in the dark swirls on the dress I'd drawn in my sketchbook. I glanced at the ovens to see if my bread was finished rising. The situation with Prince Torin and Sapphira left me perturbed.

"This is what happens when you stay asleep for twenty years, Nyx. You miss all the fun." I teased myself and darkened the sketched line on the figure's hair. Whenever I got stressed as a kid, my eldest sister Clarista would make me cook with her. She loved to create fun meals and bake delicious treats. She claimed food could solve any problem. I missed her and my family. Coming here to be of assistance to the princess brought me great joy, but I worried about my family. I had sent a messenger hawk to them yesterday, hoping they were OK.

Even as I hoped for everything to have stayed the same, I knew it wasn't. Everything was different from when I slept on that altar with Sapphira's core. I didn't regret it, and I never would. The first time I came here to visit, I knew Sapphira would play a part in something big. No clue what, but she'd make an impact, and I needed to be a part of it.

The smell of the bread had me near drooling on my sketchpad when Dris walked in. I've always liked the little owl Fae.

"I smell rosemary cheddar bread!" Dris said and floated in. Her wispy smoke-like hair and wide eyes made me smile. Although alike in some ways, I was very vocal and stubborn while she was quieter and liked to be flexible. I hoped we would become great friends.

"Yeah. Stress cooking." I set my sketches down. Dris peeked at what I'd been doing. I blushed. I wasn't the best artist in the world, but I wasn't terrible either. I liked drawing different types of Fae and outfits to match their unique personalities and appearances.

"Stress drawing, too?" She strode over to get a better look and complimented my techniques.

"Yeah. Today was a rough day for Sapphira, and I know I didn't make it better talking to Prince Torin." I wished I would have kept my mouth shut. Not that the words I said weren't true, but I kicked a male while he was down. I was better than that.

"I heard." Dris's fingers lightly followed the path of the dress like she could feel how the fabric would flow. I glanced at the oven and checked on the bread. It looked divine and the top was perfectly golden. I grabbed the oven mitts and set the pan on the top. I dusted some rosemary leaves on top and now I waited for it to cool.

"When Sapphira showed up as a human, she was in love with the prince. When I revealed information about him, her face fell, and I'd worried she would release her tears." Dris spoke from behind me and I shifted in her direction.

"She does love him. A part of her always will, but like the first time she and Rune started fighting their pull, they can't stay away from each other. She's probably feeling a magnitude of emotions right now. Guilt, shame, anger, confusion. She wants to be who she was before Verin's deceit, but that's impossible. She is someone new now, and she's got to figure out who that version of her is." Dris made several points I had surmised as well.

"I know. I just hope I can help her. I like to fix things. It's the only thing I know."

Dris nodded in understanding. "If I may make a suggestion, I think you should be there for what she needs but let her figure out her life herself. It's kind of our job as her friend. We're here to help push her crown back on her head when it slips." Dris smiled and my essence warmed from her comfort. Before the bookworm showed up, I felt out of control. Now, I felt like I was doing ok considering the circumstances.

"Thanks, Dris. I know things are out of sorts now, and I doubt we'll have a sense of normalcy soon. But I'm glad you're a part of this." I embraced her whether she was a hugger or not.

"I've heard about the rescue to get Prince Torin, but tell me everything. I know you owls see everything," I teased and watched as Dris's face lit up. We chatted about her life as Celestine's niece, and how mischievous they were together. Their relationship was more mother/daughter than with her own mother. I liked Celestine, even though she tended to be meddlesome.

"Do you have a lover?" I asked, changing the subject.

"Men in books are much better than men in reality." She took a bite of the cooled bread and moaned.

"Stop flirting with me, Dris. It's not very ladylike." A male voice entered the room and Dris's cheeks turned pomegranate red. Emrys swaggered into the room with a dazzling smirk. He wasn't my type but I could see the appeal—black hair, dark eyes, and a lip piercing on his cupid's bow lips. He dressed like a rebel and I'm fairly sure if I heard the stories right was a spy.

"I wasn't flirting. I was enjoying the precious bread." Dris sliced herself another piece of bread, then backed away slowly. "Well, I'm off to the library. I'm sure I'll see you both soon when we talk about what needs to be done." She took another bite and was off.

"She likes me. She doesn't want to admit it." Emrys shrugged and walked over to my bread.

"You made this?" he asked and helped himself to a slice. While I thought it was a bit rude to take without asking, I didn't care. I was interested in his character and might be able to chat for a few minutes if he was eating.

"I did. I like to bake when I'm dealing with stuff." I leaned against the counter and watched him. He moved without sound; his movements were quick and precise. I could see how he could get into places where he wasn't supposed to.

"I got ya. I like to eat when I'm dealing with stuff. Thanks for the bread." He patted his belly while he enjoyed his slice. I heard a noise down the hall and looked to see who would be coming into the kitchen now. No one entered and so I returned to chat with Emrys.

Only he was gone.

What an interesting group we had here. I guess I needed to figure out where I fit within this unusual circle.

Chapter Ten

Sapphira

I walked around the woods surrounding the palace until sunrise and eventually found my way to the waterfall where Rune had trained me. After seeing Desmire stick his nose through the falls to be with the queen, I knew there was a cave behind the falls. But there was another memory attached to that cave that had me holding my breath as I climbed through the pouring water to step onto a rocky ledge.

"You came." He breathed, and my knees wobbled, hearing his voice. I shouldn't be here. No one knew I was here, but I had to see for myself. I had to know what this was between us.

"I did." I searched for the scarred male in the dark but couldn't see him. The cave probably went on for miles and without a torch, I'd be screwed. The ground rumbled beneath my feet and for a moment fear licked my spine. Dying in a cave would not be pleasant.

Warm breath caressed my neck and I stilled my erratically beating heart.

"What is this?" My voice grew husky, and my fingers flexed with the yearning to touch him. I was supposed to be getting to know Prince Torin and agree to be his wife. Everyone expected it from me.

"I don't know, but it's strong." His voice tickled the hairs at the nape of my neck. I breathed deeply then faced him. Ever since that day in the Hallowstags where he attempted to rescue me, I'd been enamored by him. Rune, the cursed prince from another continent. I'd heard the stories and had often wondered where truth and rumor lay in them. Everything about him screamed opposite of his brother. Where Torin was kind, funny, and social, Rune was hard lines, body built from fighting, and scowled almost nonstop.

"I just . . ." I bit my lip, fully knowing I shouldn't say what I wanted to say. A warm, callused hand cupped my cheek, and the nerves in my body tingled in an exhilarating way.

"Say it." He leaned closer, sensed what I wanted but knew I had to be the one to voice it aloud. This thing, this attraction between us could simply be lust. My heart clenched at the thought. I lifted my head and stared into his beautiful icy eyes. I saw more than his feelings in those cool depths. I saw his beast, and I saw the other half of my soul. We moved at the same time. This dance we had been doing around each other the past month had brought us to this final moment. Once his lips connected to mine, what felt like a loose band inside me pulled tight, wrapping our fates together in destiny's tapestry.

I blinked at the cave walls, and my lips trembled. No one would hear me cry or scream here, so I released the pain and grief into the vast darkness. My heart hurt, and my muddled mind couldn't think. Destiny weighed me down, and I didn't think I could go on. As a human, I thought all I had to do was save Tor and open the onyx tomb. Then the princess could save the world while I lived in the city with Tor. Only that life was a lie. Those childhood memories were all fake. The reality was I did care for Tor, and I cared for Rune. I would even go on a limb and state I've been falling in love with the general for weeks. Our mated souls remembered each other when our heads did not. Poor Tor. I didn't mean to love him too.

I needed something to go right in my life. I needed a break, where destiny didn't have her foot on my back pushing me down. I laid on the rocky floor of the cave, shivering from my wet clothes clinging to my chilled skin until I knew Nyx could no longer cover for me. I owed her so much, and yet I knew I'd have to ask her for more. I'd have to ask all of my friends for more, and I prayed they would stand by my side. I climbed out from behind the waterfall and jumped to the ground with ease. At least I had my Fae senses again, so that was a positive.

"At least you're not falling on your ass anymore." Rune's voice entered the clearing. I shifted to see him leaning against a tree wearing a tan tunic, black pants tucked into black boots, and his trusty sword at his side.

"Lucky me." I stood still for a moment, unsure if he'd allow me close, or if we were going to talk.

"Your mother wants you." His face didn't look as pinched and rage-filled as it had the last time I saw him. However, Rune was never one to forgive easily. Once you wronged him, he cut ties. I had no idea where we stood, and I hated that. Still, I had a princess life to live now. I walked past him and swallowed the lump that formed in my throat. I'd already poured my soul onto the rocks. I could make it a few more hours without a breakdown.

Without warning, he gripped my arm and yanked me back. I turned to tell him to fuck off but his lips silenced my voice. My mate. I cried out into his mouth, and he growled. Our hands gripped wherever they could touch, and our inches of separation were too much. His tongue thrust between my lips and I matched his need with a caress of my own. I needed this . . . his strength and touch to make me feel like myself again. His fingers delved into my hair and I moaned. Suddenly, his fingers tightened and pulled my head back by my hair. He snarled then released me. He took a few steps back and I glared at him.

"I'm still pissed." And he walked toward the palace.

Instead of making things worse, I stayed silent rather than releasing the harsh words accumulating behind my lips.

Once we reached my mother's chambers, I gripped the handle tightly. "Next time you feel like kissing me, don't leave me needy or I might find another way to soothe the ache."

Rune's jaw tightened and his hands clenched into fists before he stomped away. Feeling victorious, I realized that screwing with Rune for his reactions was a staple in both the Fae and human versions of me.

I entered my mother's room with a slight blush coating my smiling cheeks. As far as I could remember, Rune and I never had sex. I tried to be as good as possible while engaged to his brother, but I hadn't been able to deny Rune's kiss.

"Moon, Moon, Moon." My mother's voice cooled the redness on my cheeks. Nothing like your mom's voice to make you stop thinking naughty thoughts.

"Hello, Mother." Everything was bright and breezy in her open chambers with sheer curtains blowing in the breeze and settling briefly on the white décor. I poured us some tea from her beautiful diamond tea set. She hummed as she took her cup. We used to converse for hours, and she never made me fear talking to her about anything. So I used the opportunity to tell her about my thoughts, even if she couldn't say something to comfort me. She was there, and watching me intently as the last of my confused feelings leaked from my soul.

Chapter Eleven

Sapphira

"Here are the maps of our realm and the human one." Dris set down the large rolls of paper in front of me.

"Great!" I helped her open them up and placed books on the curling ends.

"You doing ok?" she asked, and I nodded, eager to get started. Ever since I poured my heart out in the cave, Rune's kiss, and chatting with my mother I felt more comfortable with where I was. Everything would be ok, and I clung to that hope. Now, I wanted to get started. Soon, I'd be traveling to Crystoria but needed to know how to get there. Flying on my father would draw too much attention so horseback would be the way to go.

"I am actually." I spoke proudly considering I'd been having near constant anxiety since I changed back to Fae. Dris peered at me with her head tilted to the side. I knew she was looking for anything beneath my words, but they were true. I had no hidden issues right now.

"I'm happy you're ok." She walked around the table and hugged me. I smiled and embraced the little Fae back.

"Ok, so when Verin did whatever his mysterious action that lead to everyone's demise, he also cut our communications to Crystoria. Scouts had been sent but none returned. As our king, he said he had contact with them and gave updates on their conditions. However, knowing who he is now, I'm not sure we can trust his words on the state of the city." She walked around the table and sighed.

"What do you know about the road there?" I asked, while my gaze searched the map for the ancient road that used to lead straight there. Dris pointed to where Crysia stood, then dragged her finger toward the opposite coast of the continent.

"This way seems like the best to my knowledge. We should be able to cross in our realm straight to Crystoria and not need to enter the human realm at all."

"Best to avoid that if we can since they are probably searching for us after we torched their Iron City." I winced, knowing the cost to save Tor had been steep.

"My only concern is we don't know the state of everything in between here and Crystoria. The Harold's Temple is there." She pointed to a desert area, then dragged her finger to a chasm. "This is Rainfall's Deep, and if the bridge is broken, we can't cross it. The ride around would add five days to our trip."

I crossed my fingers, hoping the road ahead was intact. "Anything else we need to keep an eye out for?" I focused on the map, but no memories of the land before me stood out. I recognized a lot on the human map, which made me slightly more confident going that route than the Fae one. There was a reason we protected the humans from the creatures in our realm. A lot of those creatures lived outside this city, and they wouldn't growl twice before eating us.

Dris whistled to herself as she ran through the knowledge in her head. "I don't think so. Just those two things. Harold's Temple used to be a place of worship, but it became a haven for Fae gone crazy and I'd hate to capture their attention if they are still alive."

She shivered and flashbacks of the demented Dramens rushed through my mind. I didn't plan on running into them, either. "OK. Sounds like a plan. We'll need to study both of these maps, then draft a timeline. I'll see who will join me on this crazy mission." I stood and clapped my hands together. Now I was getting somewhere, and felt like I could check something off my list of things to accomplish.

"I'm coming. Of course, you would be completely lost without me." Dris grinned as she looked over the maps with eager eyes. She would no doubt have everything memorized by morning.

"I'm glad you're my friend. Thank you for everything you did before, and well . . . not treating me differently."

"Pishh. You're still you. Only now you have a bigger room for us to hang out in."

I laughed and shook my head. "You love me for my bigger room and not my big heart. I see where your loyalties are."

"Oh yes, that's exactly why I went with you to that horrid city and will travel with you again. Your big rooms." She winked as wind rattled the stained glass of the library.

"It's going to be a cold journey." Winters in the Fae realm were different and crueler than the human side. We couldn't wait until the weather warmed. We'd wear warm clothes and make fires around camp to fight the chill.

When we finished studying the maps, I headed to the arena to train and work on weapons skills. Since I didn't remember everything I could do before. Power hummed beneath my skin and I rested against the beam of the weapons shelter as my vision swirled. The magic within me stirred. I hadn't touched that chasm of power within me for fear I couldn't control it. Memories floated in my mind of me using each unique gift I'd absorbed. However, I was apprehensive . . . I didn't want to rely on them, either.

Najen continued to help me grow with the passing hours, and his teaching method calmed me. He made me laugh, as did his husband when he came into the ring from the artisan part of the city for a visit. Rojan and Najen were cute together. Najen was tough and brawny while Rojan's blond hair and warm brown eyes piled on top of a smaller frame body made him look so sweet. Rojan was an optimist that believed anyone could do anything if the person believed it themselves. He was a painter in the city, where they had both lived together for the last 25 years.

"Don't worry, Sapphira, the general will come around." Najen bumped me on the shoulder with his while his husband nodded. I wanted to ask if they were mates,

56

but after spending twenty minutes with them I had my answer. I could see that everlasting bond between them with every smile and touch they gave one another. I wonder if Rune and I looked like that.

"Thanks." We chatted for another thirty minutes about their relationship, and how it was hard for Rojan to see his husband battle in the fight against Verin's soldiers on the day magic disappeared. He'd been hurt, but only a scar claimed his back instead of death at his throat. After saying goodbye, I walked around the gardens with a contagious smile on my face. I had nothing on the agenda and everyone seemed to be giving me free time today to do as I pleased. I briefly wondered if Nyx barked orders at people to give me space. I loved my friends.

I nodded at the guards I passed by and watched the birds fly as the sun set on our day.

"Celestineee." A cool breeze called to me, and I looked up to see my feet had taken me to Celestine's cave.

Chapter Twelve

Sapphira

I followed the dark cave path to where Celestine sat by her fire in the familiar woods, with tea and food ready for me.

"This tea isn't laced with your blood and opal is it?" I sat in the grass and tossed a grape into my mouth. Celestine's owl eyes shifted to me and a mischievous smile tilted her lips.

"It's lavender and honey, my dear."

I lifted the cup to my nose and sniffed it for anything odd. She'd used that other blend on me so I would have visions and memories to help move me closer to my destiny of becoming Fae again. Rune liked to call her a meddlesome old hag, but she'd been helpful to me.

"Meo-hoo." One of her strange owl cats twisted its head toward me. They were sort of cute, although I wouldn't have one as a pet. I couldn't find anything strange about the scent of the tea, so I took a sip and nothing but the ingredients she said coated my tongue.

"So quiet, Sapphira. Having troubles?" She sat on a large branch across from her fire and her owl cats surrounded her. Some purred and others hooted, with their tails twitching from side to side.

"I'm doing better. I should have come for some of that calming tea you gave me before now." After the words came out, I wanted to kick myself for not having thought of that before. I would have been much more relaxed than I have been.

"You're doing fine. Everything is coming together nicely."

"I hope so."

She knew everything I wanted to say, and what would happen. She had set everything in motion with my fate. From telling my parents how to protect me from Verin, then she sent Tor to rescue me.

"I was starting to fear that I wasn't the old me again, but I wasn't human, either." I sipped some tea and tore off the piece of bread she had set on the plate for me with honey drizzled on top.

"You are a new you, and only you can decide who you are."

I nodded, having come to the same conclusion. I didn't have time to try to be like any of the old versions of me. I began to accept who I was in this moment.

"I know you can't give me anything that could change the course of destiny, but do you have any words of wisdom on what's to come?" I asked.

"You were always my favorite royal." Her whispery voice sounded like a purr and she grinned sweetly. I sipped on the tea and waited to hear any clues as to what my future held for me.

"Bring that handsome mate of yours to see me, and I'll tell you what I can. I would like to see his face. It's been some time." She scratched the ear of one of her pets, and I sighed. As the princess, I could call Rune here and he'd have to come, but that didn't mean he wanted to.

"You sure you don't want his grumpiness to mess up your comfy space?" I semi teased, mostly because I wasn't sure I wanted to face him after what I said to him last. Warmth stirred in my belly as the thoughts of his kiss rushed through my head.

"He spent many days with me after you left twenty years ago. He begged, willing to do anything to save you. I told him that he had to wait and wait he did. I haven't seen him since. Bring him, my dear. Let me look into his soul, and then we'll talk."

She disappeared with a fog in true Celestine fashion. Curiosity had me wanting to follow her into the dark woods and search for where her true home was. This fire pit was a front . . . a place where people could chat with her without being in her sanctuary. I ate the rest of the honey bread and finished my tea.

As I headed back to the palace, I asked the first guard I saw, "Hey, have you seen General Rune?" He shook his head while remaining tight-lipped. I walked around the palace, hoping to catch him stomping nearby but he wasn't in sight. A flutter tickled my stomach as déjà vu hit me when I stopped in front of his quarters. The last time I had approached his wooden door, he'd been shirtless, and I'd wished he was mine while he belonged to another.

I sighed deeply, then rapped my knuckles against the sturdy door. I didn't hear any movements, so I leaned my ear against the wood and listened just in case he chose to ignore me. With my attention focused on the room beyond the barrier, I didn't hear the swift footsteps of someone until my hands were pinned above my head, and my body squished between the hard surface and a body.

"What do you want?" Rune's harsh voice vibrated against my ear. The stubble on his jaw scratched against my neck and I shivered.

"I need you to come with me to Celestine's cave." I tried to speak without sounding breathless, however I wasn't sure I accomplished such feat. Rune's chest rumbled behind me and his fingers slipped between mine almost painfully against the wood.

"Why?" His body molded to mine and an intense need crashed into me. I pressed my backside into his front and his snarl against the side of my hair ripped a moan from my lips. An unfortunate truth to my new life was technically being a forty-two-year-old woman who'd only had sex two times before him and had possibly reached my quota of sexual tension to last all my immortal years. My mate's body flexed behind me, and I felt the length of him stir in his pants.

"She has intel about the future, and she is willing to give but wants to see you first." The words rushed as I continued to shamelessly rock myself against his hardness. He was mine, and I'd always been hopeless whenever we were close like this.

"Fine. Let's go." His words were short and gave no indication he was aroused. Without the evidence pressing into my ass, I'd have assumed he didn't want me. Rune pulled away, and stomped toward the exit that led to Celestine.

Chapter Thirteen

Rune

No self-control.

I'm pissed and betrayal runs thick in my blood with every heartbeat. Yet, when I see her, I need to be with her . . .to feel her, know her, claim her. Seeing her leaning against my door drove me wild with need. I wanted to yank her inside my room and—

I shut down all thoughts of what I'd do with her. I didn't know what I wanted right now. To claim her or fight her, both seemed viable. Especially since she wore those tight human pants that hugged every curve of her ass. The beast within me whined. He wanted his mate, and she was so close. Sapphira stomped behind me to the meddlesome hag's cave. If the seer would willingly part with information about what's to come, then I had no choice.

The tunnels to her fire pit were decorated with drawings of the past. Memories I tried to repress daily hit me with every step closer to Celestine.

"How do I get her out?" I growled at the seer. She knew. I know she did. I'd been here every damn day and she gave me the same damn answer.

"Such fire within you, Prince. Good, you're going to need it." She purred and scratched her pet's ears. She had set out tea and a plate full of food and I kicked it over like I had every day I came into this haunted place. I wanted my mate out of that damn onyx, not tea and berries.

"You need to rest and have patience. She will be released when the time is right." She said those words so calmly . . . like I hadn't been patient for a whole year. I barely sleep, my chest felt so tight like I can't breathe, let alone control the blinding rage inside me.

"I need my mate." I snarled and paced the well-worn grass from previous days.

"Prince Rune, no amount of snarling will change what is. I suggest you take the queen's offer to be general and find purpose until the princess is released. She is going to need you by her side more than anyone once she returns. No weapons can destroy the onyx, as you know. One day someone will find our city and will save her. Until then, patience young prince." Celestine's strained voice sounded like she wished to tell me more.

I collapsed to the ground, the weight of defeat pulling me down. I would never stop loving her, never stop trying to save her from that cursed tomb.

"Then I shall wait."

Twenty years I waited for the princess to be rescued. I took no other females since my heart, my beast, and my body belonged to her. She owned me, cursed soul and all. I glanced at the princess as we stepped into the clearing where two plates and cups of tea sat gently on the

"Great plan, but did you schedule in mishaps and trouble?" Emrys asked, his surprisingly serious tone making me suppress a giggle. I sometimes forgot that the goat Fae was blood bound to me and took being a part of the team very seriously, even though he liked to joke around.

"I did. In fact, I stretched out the itinerary with spaces for trouble, extra rest, and detours." She coughed, then muttered quickly, "You could have read that on the calendar, but that's apparently too hard for you."

Everyone but Ryka and Rune burst into a fit of laughter after her sneaky snide comment. Even Emrys grinned like a fool at the owl Fae. He loved ruffling her feathers. Dris moved on and started talking about the route we would take and the dangers involved . . . the temple, the bridge, and what to expect for those who hadn't been to Crystoria. The more she delved into the tiniest of details she had gathered from her books, the more at ease I felt. Would there be dangers ahead? Undoubtedly. However, the details let me believe I had a sense of control of what lay ahead.

"The only thing left to do is pack for the trip, which I can make a list of supplies and get rides ready. I know Desmire is staying behind to help protect Crysia with the queen." Dris looked at Ryka who nodded underneath her white-and-blue hood.

"Good. Can't have Verin attacking while we are away. Desmire is a great fiery deterrent." Nyx spoke for the first time since we sat down, and everyone glanced at her. She blushed and went back to being silent, which was odd, since Nyx never had any issues using her voice.

"I sort of feel silly for asking, but who is going with me on this journey?" I assumed everyone besides Ryka, but I needed to hear it officially.

"Definitely a silly question. I'm going." Emrys nudged my shoulder and I pushed right back. One by one, my group sounded off their vows to go. Even Nyx, who didn't care for long journeys. She usually liked to stay in the palace instead of play in the woods. However, she'd been inside that tomb for twenty years, maybe she wanted to see the world and experience what she'd missed.

Rune had given me his vow last night and remained silent now. Everyone in the room knew he'd be joining us, though.

"OK. Does anyone need mode of transportation?" Dris grabbed a pen and a small notebook, then waited for anyone to answer her. I thought about my old horse, Serphan, but she had been a regular horse and would have died. I glanced to Ryka, remembering how she offered to take me across the continent with Mariam with her power to jump the realm just before Verin's evil deeds. I could have ridden my horse, but my parents wanted me as far away from the castle as quickly as possible.

"I do," I said and watched Dris scribble on her pad.

"I do, too." Nyx joined me, and I glanced at her with a soft smile. Her horse had been normal and would

"I'm not a shiny toy to fight over. I don't care about the history between you. Or with me. I'm a completely different person than in your memories. I'm not the princess or human Sapphira of the past and I don't have time for this. We're leaving in three days and you boys will come to a truce. Right now." I stepped into the fire and purred as its silk-like tendrils caressed against me. Tor watched me with wide eyes and I'm sure I looked like a psycho woman standing inside the fire with a grin on my face. A few seconds later, his expression changed into that familiar, easygoing Tor I'd stared at countless times.

"All right, you can quit with the theatrics. I'll be nice and stop raising his hackles on purpose." Tor's hand thrust forward, waiting for Rune to step up and accept the agreement. Rune stood, his gaze shifting from Tor's hand to me. His face held no shock or anger in his relaxed features. Instead his focus seemed dazzled. Like he'd walk right into these flames and kiss me. I wanted him to.

"Fine." He walked over and shook Tor's hand.

"Now, if you'll excuse me, I have a ball to get ready for." I flicked my wrist and the flames disappeared. As much as I wanted to stare at my hands and make pretty fire again, I cared about making a dramatic exit more. I strutted to the entrance of the castle like the badass goddess I was, giggling the entire way.

"Who's the goddess?" I opened the door to my room and waited for the praise. Nyx was surely watching the whole showdown from the window.

"That was pretty warrior princess of you. I'm impressed." She gave me a slow clap and I curtsied.

"Hopefully, their truce will last the whole journey. I'm not holding my breath though. Tor is one joke away from Rune lunging for him." I twirled myself to the bathroom where my bath awaited.

"Oh for sure. No way those two can keep being nice forever. It's against their nature. Even before you, they were like opposite sides of a magnet." Nyx glanced out the window and then closed it. I stepped into the hot bath, scents of lemongrass wafting in the air and my body relaxed. Putting the brothers in their place made me feel unstoppable. I lifted my hand above the water and willed fire to spring from my fingertips. Little orange flames shot out and lit the curtain on fire.

"Shit!" I jumped up and splashed as much water as I could to douse the blaze. Smoke billowed out of the bathroom and Nyx came running in, ready to save me.

"Looks like you're going to need a little more practice using your powers again, Princess." She laughed and I sank into the water, wishing I could drown myself from the embarrassment. So much for being a badass.

"I'll get new ones hung up before the night is over. I'm thinking a pale blue would really bring the wood coloring out more." Nyx ignored the blush on my cheeks and went into decorating mode.

After I had soaked in the large tub, I donned a curve-hugging, red, showstopping, lacy dress. Nyx quickly made me look presentable then rushed to get ready didn't feel intense need myself. Suddenly, screams echoed off the palace walls. We jumped apart and ran without thought to the main event, only to be met by three soldiers in red-and-black armor. Verin's men.

"We come bearing gifts for the resurrected princess." I withdrew my sword and walked toward them. Sapphira slowly moved to her mother, and the guards stationed around her. These three men had snuck in undetected. Najen and I would have to do a thorough search of our defenses for failure. Twice they had invaded our land while I'd been distracted. It wouldn't happen again.

"General Wolfstrom." The man with pale blue skin stepped forward which singled him as the leader in the group.

"State your business before we arrest you," I calmly demanded, despite the anger bubbling inside me. Not only had they ruined my time with Sapphira, they were here. That was insult enough.

"King Verin selected a special gift for the princess since word of her return has reached all the lands." He kneeled and held out an intricately carved box made of black wood. I nudged it open with my sword and bile rose in my throat. A few of the women screamed from the sight of the rotting head of a woman who resembled Sapphira in appearance. Maggots wiggled over her lifeless eyes, and dried blood coated the satin material the head laid upon.

"A gift and a warning. Stay here in your palace and we can be peaceful. Attempt to return magic and it will be your head gifted to your mother next time." The man laughed, and I reacted instinctually. I lunged on silent feet and my blade swiftly found the weakness in his armor, severing his head from his body. I turned to fight the other two but they collapsed to the ground, blue foam leaking from their mouths as they convulsed.

"The ball is over. Go back to your homes," I announced and nodded at the guards stationed with the queen and Sapphira. Connor, the young warrior who outranked the others, nodded. Sapphira's stare burned against my skin as the warrior guided them inside, but she needed to go. I needed her safe and away from this mess to focus on my job.

"General, they slaughtered our three guards stationed on the west side of the realm gates." Commander Najen appeared with heavy breaths.

"Notify the families, and return the dead. We don't rest tonight until this shit is cleaned up, and our city is safe again. Take beta unit and search for possible attack points. They chose that spot for a reason. I want to know how they got there." They quickly did as they were told, while two soldiers stepped up to dispose of the dead men in the grass.

"Take them to healer Rista. I want to know what poison they took."

Lastly my gaze fell on the woman's head that had rolled out of the box and stared with those dead eyes at the stars. Part of me wished Sapphira would heed Verin's warning, at least then she might stay safe. However,

Verin's threat would only spur her to bring magic back to defeat him more. I'd be there to aide her and protect her, and I'd be damned if I'd let that slimy prick of a jing lay a hand on her wild brown curls.

Chapter Seventeen

Sapphira

"Even though pushing the timeline up two days was challenging, I think I managed." Dris walked down the hallway to the throne room with a big bag over her shoulder.

"Thank you. We needed to get a move on before Verin came up with another way to threaten me." I placed a hand on her shoulder for a few seconds. She really came through for me this time, and so many before now. I loved my friend very much.

After Verin's threat last night, I sent messages to everyone that we would be leaving the following morning. No one demanded we wait. They all agreed after seeing the unsettling display of a woman's head that looked like me in the box.

"There are some choice animals down in the stables you'll have to choose from to ride on the journey. Horses, unicorns, catagaro, rhinothesins, and a few wolfawks." She winked and I grinned. I remembered what most of those looked like, but the details were fuzzy.

Nyx, Emrys, Tor, and Rune all stood in the stables with their rides and many bags. We were in for a long journey.

"Whoa, look at you, warrior princess," I said to Nyx. Her thick pants were tucked into knee-high brown boots, and her leather long-sleeved top flowed over her backside like a tuxedo—short in the front, long in the back. I noticed diamond armor peeking out from her cinched shirt. Even in armor, Nyx outshone the highest fashion critiques. Her lavender hair was braided to the side and a pair of duel swords were attached to her back.

"Can't arrive in Crystoria looking like a troll now can I?" She stuck out her tongue and pat the head of a beautiful creature. It looked like a horse, only it had dark brown antlers. Golden swirls ran along its thick neck and glowed when its hair brushed against them.

"She's beautiful. Are you riding her?" The horse nodded and I stood there in awe.

"Yeah, I walked by her earlier and she nearly kicked the door right off. She chose me, and I am honored." Nyx's fingers caressed the creature's antlers and it purred. How intriguing.

"You think that creature is beautiful, wait until you see my Jengo." Emrys walked around the back of the stable then returned with a large mountain goat-looking animal. It was the size of a bear with layers of thick black wool and two large curling horns.

"I'm impressed." I walked past the others and pet the large goat, which huffed.

"I snagged all the weapons Rune allowed and a few more." He winked and I chuckled. Of course he grabbed more, and I'm sure Rune knew about them too. But with my life at stake, he would turn a blind eye to Emerys grabbing extra in order to protect us. Thoughts of Rune made my cheeks turn pink and I glanced around until I found him standing next to an oversized bear.

"He's starting to warm up to me, which is good considering I'm your best friend and we can't have a man coming between us." Emrys teased me, and his humor would be needed on those days where the weight of our mission became too much.

"We definitely can't have that." I patted him on the shoulder before walking toward my mate. I greeted Tor as he threw a saddle on his unicorn, and he smiled at me before focusing on his tasks. Rune tossed a bedroll, and a leather bag on the side of the bluish, black bear.

"Is it yours?" I asked and stood within two feet from them both. The bear shifted its head toward me and knocked Rune out of the way with its large backside and nuzzled my face with its wet nose.

"Yeah, he's my pain in the ass." Rune nudged the creature from my face and I laughed.

"I don't remember him from before."

"Silvio found me about nine years ago. Besides a few horses, most animals are edgy around me. My other nature disturbs them." Rune caressed the leather covering my torso, while gazing at my armor and knee-high boots.

"I missed seeing you in armor."

Thoughts of kissing him with only select pieces of armor on our bodies coursed through my mind. His low voice did that to me. "You do look mighty sexy all dressed for a fight." I stepped two inches closer and his low growl startled the animals.

"Sapphira, you're pushing it." He took a step back at an attempt to remain in control in front of everyone.

"I'm not pushing anything . . . yet." I shifted so the others couldn't see me before I ran my hand over the general's armor-covered torso, then down, down. Quicker than a lightning strike, Rune's hand snatched mine and held it close to his lips. He didn't say a word and I shivered from the intensity radiating from his icy-blue eyes. His mouth pressed a hard kiss against my skin and that shiver shook a soft moan past my throat. The ground shook, and we both glanced to the open area of the stables where Ryka walked alongside my mother and father toward our location.

"Soon, Princess." Rune leaned down, the scruff against his jaw scratching the side of my cheek as he whispered in my ear. That I believed. Rune had never been a man that withheld his thoughts or desires from me. He may be standoffish with everyone else, but with me, he'd been real. Even when we tried to squash our feelings for each other, I could feel them in every look.

Desmire rumbled, and I put distance between my mate and me.

"Moon gifts ruby, stars are blinding." Mother lifted her arms as she walked into the stable and I ran into them.

My friends bowed at her presence before continuing to ready their creatures for departure.

"I'm going to miss you so much. I promise I'll be safe and return magic to you." I hoped magic could heal her mind and make her whole again. A large snout bumped us and we leaned against my father's dragon head in one family embrace. I just got them back only to leave them again.

"Take care of her," I whispered to my father, and his scaled face nodded against us. Tears fell from my mother's serene face as she stared off. I couldn't fail. I just couldn't. We pulled apart and Mother walked toward the animals with a smile on her face. She loved to visit the stables with me in my younger days and teach me that even though we rode them and treated them as pets, it was only because they allowed us the honor. We did not control nature. We worked together in symbiosis.

A loud roar echoed around the building and everyone stood guard.

"Your mother's gift to you for your journey." Ryka clasped her hand in mine and walked me toward a jungle setting in the stable. Each stall had been created to make the creature feel at home and opened to wide fields and woods. A ten-foot-tall cat-like creature stood proudly and growled as we approached. Its desert-colored fur looked soft, and its long, pointed ears shifted at our arrival.

"A catagaro." I placed my hand against the wooden gate in awe. I remembered these creatures now. They were fast and swift. Nothing in our realm was faster or

"I think that's a great idea. I can help, too. We all can." Dris clapped and rattled off training ideas and testing Sapphira's strengths.

"I can't wait to get my powers back," Emrys said, and everyone stopped talking. It had been twenty years since the Fae had access to their gifts and their nature cores. Not a day past that you couldn't feel that missing power within.

"What would you do?" Dris asked curiously and without her usual disdain for Emrys laced in her voice.

Emrys smirked while stoking the fire with a long stick. "Cause a little mischief." He winked but Dris didn't let him off that easy.

"You have the power to turn invisible, and that's what you choose?" She scoffed, and Sapphira choked on her food. "Invisible! Holy cow Emrys, that's so cool. I'd walk around naked in front of everyone if I could be invisible." Sapphira laughed and when Rune and I made the same scowling faces, she laughed even harder.

"I mean that was a given." Emrys reached his hand to the side to high-five the princess and Dris, who reluctantly slapped her hand against his.

"I'm going to go for a long flight. I miss feeling the wind against my feathers." Dris gleamed, her eyes glazed with thoughts of flying. The forest wind stood still as everyone was heavy in their own thoughts. Life without magic was a life without half a soul. It's who we were, even me, a half Fae half human prince. Instead of continuing the weighted talk of dreams, I chose humor.

101

"When I get my powers back, I'm going to finally get the truth from Nyx about how she's hopelessly in love with me."

Nyx's eyes narrowed. Yeah, I chose her for my jest because I enjoyed causing that face of hers to pinch up. Sapphira, Emerys, and Dris laughed. I had the power to know if people were telling the truth or not. A common knowledge amongst the kingdom that spread before I arrived.

"You're going to hear the truth about something, but it won't be that." Nyx huffed and drank from her cup while staring into the woods. I had pissed her off, but everyone else appeared to be in a better mood. I'd say it was a fair trade.

"What about you, Rune?" Sapphira asked, to bring my brother into the conversation. Rune's power was over the earth, as well as controlling his werewolf side. My father feared him and shunned him for those gifts. Claiming me to be his rightful heir to the throne. I played the politics games with my gifts, while Rune became a soldier. I'd often felt like Rune would have made a better king than me, but whenever I tried to make my feelings known, he'd shut them down.

"Probably knock out a mountain, huh?" I blurted, before I realized I sounded hopeful. I mentally cursed myself and shrugged like I hadn't sounded like a kid who idolized his older brother. Once upon a time I'd looked up to him, but as I'd aged I realized he chose to remain an asshole, and didn't want to change. Rune pursed his lips and I waited for some form of grumble from him, but then he surprised me. "Sounds good."

Sapphira smiled next to him and a small corner of my own lips lifted. He didn't snarl at my talking to him. Maybe the truce between us could really dig deep.

"All right crew, I think story time is over for now. We have a schedule to keep if we want to reach Crystoria in seventeen days." Dris stood and urged everyone to get ready. I'd already packed up our tent, so I helped the girls with their belongings.

"I don't need your help." Nyx grabbed the neatly organized bags to take to the animals. There was still work to be done whether she wanted my help or not, so I got to work on breaking down their tent and rolling up the bed mats.

"Sorry if I offended you with my joke. The group needed a little laugh."

"Right. Are you done?" She stood with her foot thumping against the grass, and her arms crossed over her chest.

"Yeah, I'm done." I hoisted the remaining bags and carried them to the creatures. Nyx watched me with a pensive scowl until Dris demanded her attention.

"She's always been a bit of a bitch. Don't let it bother you." The gruff voice of my brother came from my right. Dare I admit that his words appeared to show he cared about my feelings?

"Yeah," I mumbled and tried not to read too much into the interaction. But as we left camp, I couldn't help but feel maybe this journey would change us in more ways than one. Magic would be returned, and maybe . . . I'd know what it was like to have a brother who cared.

Chapter Twenty - One

Sapphira

I remember the last time I trekked this route. The scenery had been vastly different. My mother and the Queen of Crystoria got together once a year. Usually they switched locations to visit each other's kingdom. Travelers would wave as we passed with soldiers riding behind us. There were minor villages scattered along the road that we could stop at to rest and chat with the people.

This time, the road was in ruins as were the villages. An eerie silence surrounded us as we slowly rode through the deserted area. What happened to the people? The grass thinned into a desert landscape as we crossed into a different territory, far beyond Crysia's borders. I was grateful that we were in this realm where the Dramens couldn't hunt us. However, chills sneaked up my spine and a thick weight settled in my belly. Something wasn't right. I didn't know if it was the abandoned villages or a nearby threat giving me the foreshadowing sensations.

"Let's pick up the pace. Something doesn't feel right," Dris whispered as her gaze shifted around nervously. I lightly nudged my beast that I'd named Cara to move faster. The hackles on her neck rose, and I reached for one of the axes at my side.

Naturally, as if they'd been practicing for this moment, the boys of our group broke into formation. Rune went to the front, closest to me. Emrys and Tor positioned on our flanks, with one hand on the reins of their creatures and the other on a weapon.

"Smell that?" Rune sniffed the air and I tried to smell whatever scent he did, but his wolf side gave him an advantage. The only scents I recognized were dirt and hot, stale air.

"What is it?" I whispered and he put a calloused finger to his lips for silence. We rode for ten more minutes before we all clenched our noses from Rune's mystery smell. A solider dressed in black-and-red armor was skewered on a spear. His rotting flesh looked cooked from the hot sun, and the sound of one of our group vomiting their lunch made me cringe.

"What do you think happened to him?" Nyx broke our silence and I glanced back at her pale face and then Dris's sweating forehead before she wretched the last of her meal beside her beast.

"My guess is Verin sent scouts to the various paths to Crystoria and this one met his end. We should be wary of who else roams these lands. I suggest we stay silent until camp and keep our weapons close." Rune nudged his giant bear onward without remorse. I hated Verin, and his soldiers had been bred to remain vile and loyal only to him. They would willingly die for him, but wasn't that what

106

against him and I gasped. We shouldn't be flirting like this with one of our own missing.

"I think we will find more traps for us inside, where the good stuff would have been locked away, heavily guarded by the stone." Dris stepped toward us and Rune's lips disappeared from their familiar spot on my skin.

"Agreed." I reluctantly took a step away from my mate and went with Dris to the immense temple. Blush leaked onto my cheeks as I sensed the stare of my friend.

"You two seem to be getting along better," said the woman who could sleep all night with chaos around her but didn't miss a damn thing while she was awake.

"He can't resist my charm, the poor warrior." I evaded the statement for now, intent on searching for a way to get into the temple and to find Emrys.

Chapter Twenty - Three

Rune

"I cannot get over the feeling something strange happened here," Dris said, as I pushed open the temple doors with ease. Uneasy thoughts played in my mind as we walked into the sandy, rock floors. I took the lead and scanned the walls for any triggers.

"It is odd this place was abandoned. I remember the group to be a dedicated people. They wouldn't leave under any circumstances. My mother tried to get them to leave many times." Sapphira reached out to touch a red rock statue of a woman wrapped in flames. I reached out to stop her but she shrugged me off.

Infuriating princess.

Rumors said the people of this temple went mad . . . mad enough to create various killing pitfalls for intruders. I picked up a rock near my boot and chucked it into the room. Nothing happened as it flew through the air and landed.

"All right, look around with haste. The quicker we can get out of here, the better." I pushed my sword into its scabbard on my hip. I peered into the various jars on a table near a dais with a mosaic of the sun behind it. Nothing. The people had left and taken everything with them. Sapphira and Dris huffed as their searches amounted to nothing as well.

"The art is quite stunning for the age."

"I'll pass. They have another dark pit up here. Ugh, it's probably where they made their sacrifices to the sun." Sapphira groaned and I strode to her side. The beast inside me growled looking into the vast nothingness. That side of me only came close to the edge when my mate was around or if there was a threat.

"Whoooo enters my temple?" A hissing noise echoed through the darkness below. I nudged Sapphira behind me and stepped backward toward the door. Dris squeaked and unsheathed her bow, then docked an arrow quickly.

"We were just leaving," I called out to whoever was in there, ready to bolt with both girls over my shoulder.

"Do you see the sun at night, weary travelers?" The sound of the voice grew closer as we slowly walked away. My eyes narrowed at the rim of the pit when black fingers reached over the side and dug into the rock.

"Go," I whispered to the girls and they picked up their pace.

"You remind me of Harold. Are you him? It's been so long." Four red eyes peeked over the pit walls and I unleashed my sword. I'd fight this creature if I had to.

"I am not!" I bellowed to the creature as it slithered out of the darkness, one scaly inch at a time. The torso was that of a woman, but on her lower half a giant snake tail curled around the dais.

"When the poison spread across the land, the people turned on each other. Raping and feasting on flesh of their kind. Such sins, such atrocities the Fae committed against nature." The creature's head shifted from side to side, and her red eyes narrowed at our retreating forms. She hissed loudly. Her hand shot out and grabbed a rope I hadn't noticed on the wall before. The doors behind us closed instantly, and we were stuck with this creature in the temple with only three windows of light to help us see.

"Who are you?" Sapphira stepped around me.

"I am the real guardian of this temple. I'd allowed Harold to create his place of worship here, and he fed me to keep the peace between us, until that changed. Greed and anger corrupted their souls. That cursed shiny rock as their new god." The snake woman screamed and smacked a chair that had been falling apart against the wall. Its shattering wood echoed around the open room.

"Poison. Did this happen twenty years ago?" Sapphira stepped closer, and I wrapped my free arm around her to keep her from doing something stupid like getting close enough for the creature to strike.

"Yesssss. Twenty years. The people of the sun betrayed me. I ate them and chased the away from this sacred ground of my sisters." She lifted her hands to her hair and I noticed it dripped like oil onto the ground.

"You're one of the Vipereans aren't you?" Dris strode to stand next to me, her arrow still pointed at the creature.

"Yesss. The last and so very hungry." The snake woman swerved a foot toward us, and I pulled Sapphira back a step.

"We wouldn't be very tasty," Dris announced and I scowled at her words. She shouldn't antagonize the woman.

"I like your fire. It will taste like a drop of the sun inside my stomach." She whipped her tail in our direction and Dris fired her arrow. It slammed into the tip of the snake tail before it could hit us.

"Where did the people go?" Sapphira tried to wrestle free of my grip, and I growled for her to stop. She could risk her own damn life another time. She was no match for this creature with her limited powers. She wasn't quick or skilled enough yet to kill it.

"My dinner is talking too much," the Viperean hissed and I felt her sentiment. Sapphira was talking too much in this scenario.

"Where did they go?" Sapphira's skin grew hot and flames rose from her hands. I released her immediately and readied my feet to lunge for the Viperean.

"I did not follow them, but the winds say they followed that shiny rock. I do not know where it grows. Harold and his bride of shiny rocks. They sit on a throne of the bones of their high priests and eat the hearts of their dead. Now, it's time to eat your hearts." The creature's arms stretched out and thick white fangs dripped as she hissed at us.

The flames on Sapphira turned blue, and Dris released another arrow aimed at the human-like torso.

The creature screamed, then collapsed to the ground, a shiny blade peeking through her chest beside Dris's arrow.

"You do not want to know what's down there. This thing had a major skull fetish," a strong voice hollered behind the dead Viperean.

Sapphira's flames disappeared, and Dris dropped her bow to the ground as our gazes landed on a bloody and dirt-covered Emrys.

"But it's too easy." He bit back a laugh and I hissed in his direction. So much for coming up here to have a heart-to-heart with him.

"If you want to kiss these lips again, I won't hear a peep about my dramatics." I pointed at him as I stood, shifting my attention to the landscape. The view was breathtaking, even in the dimmed crescent moonlight. "No matter how many times I travel, I'm still in awe of how beautiful the land is." I changed the topic.

"I always preferred the land over palace life." A chilly breeze wafted by and I shivered. Rune had a good idea roosting up here. Not only did it give him a great vantage point, but these rocks baked all day in the sun. They heated my backside as I relaxed next to Rune's extra warmth.

"Me, too." From what I remembered, both Fae versions of me liked the outdoors. The human side had wanted a life of luxury since I had never experienced it before.

Silence grew between us, and while that wasn't unnatural, I wanted to talk tonight. I just didn't quite know how to express what I felt.

"I can tell you have something on your mind, Sapphira. You're picking at your fingernails and gnawing on your lip. Just spit it out."

My gaze shot to my fingers and I had indeed picked at the edges of them. Poor nails.

"I don't exactly know what I'm feeling. Sorry, I know that makes no sense." I exhaled loudly and continued to damage my nails. We were silent again before he broke it, and the last of my walls.

"About nine months ago, I woke up from a nightmare where you were being hunted and I couldn't find you." He sighed and looked up to the moon. I watched him. My hands stopped their picking as I waited to hear the rest of this story he'd chosen to share with me. Rune rarely let himself be so vulnerable, so I cherished every moment he let me in.

"I knew you were safe in that tomb, but still . . . I saddled up Silvio and left Crysia for two weeks. I had no clue what I was looking for, but something deep inside my core begged me to find what was missing. Eventually, the fear of straying too far from the tomb pulled me back to the palace."

I'd stopped moving, and I'm pretty sure I stopped breathing for the minutes he spoke. Nine months ago the community I'd lived in was attacked. I watched Mariam be brutalized and murdered. I'd experienced sheer terror and survived on my own for three months after that until Tor found me.

"I know." He reached out to cup my cheeks with his warmed hands.

"I think I felt you . . . your fear . . . even when my mind thought you were trapped in the onyx. I searched for the missing piece of my soul. I searched for you."

My breathing resumed and I rushed to tell him about my similar experience. "Right before I arrived in Crysia, I'd felt you, too. I couldn't put a name to the missing feeling in my heart, but I knew something big existed there before. Something intense, like an unyielding force that beckoned to be reunited again." My hands closed around his as he cradled my face, and I knew I'd choose this warrior—this strong, loyal, determined, and beautiful man before me—over and over.

"Rune, I—"

His lips stopped me from speaking my heart's truth. I'd claim him as mine in every life.

"You're mine," he growled as his mouth pressed hot kisses down my throat, then back to my lips again. I prayed to the Heart Tree we searched for that nothing would interrupt us this time. His hands left my face only to lift me onto his lap. Those strong fingers dug into my ass, and a moan escaped from my chest. We ravaged each other's mouths on top of that boulder but it wasn't enough. I needed more, so much more. I gripped his black hair as I kissed those three scars that ran down the side of his face. A rumble vibrated from deep inside him as I nibbled against his long neck and bobbing Adam's apple. Suddenly, my back was slammed against the warm rock with Rune's body pressed against mine. My unpinned leg wrapped around his hips as I clutched the leather on his bicep.

As far as my memories allowed, this heavy kissing and grinding was as far as we'd ever gone. Before, we'd tried to be respectful to Tor, to hold off until Rune and I could exchange vows. But that life didn't exist anymore. However, I didn't want to have sex on a boulder with our friends sleeping ten yards away, but only because I feared what might happen when I fully let loose. I couldn't control my powers, and I didn't know if I could control my voice, either.

"If I recall, sweet Princess, you demanded I not leave you needy after I've lit the fire within you." Rune lifted his head. His gaze roamed over my body; my wild hair spread against the stone surface. I knew where he was going with this and I lifted my hips into the hard length of him. He smirked and leaned down a breath's distance from my lips. I tried to press my mouth against his, but he moved back an inch to keep the teasing inch between us.

"Are you needy, Princess?" His rough purr made me want to thrash and to scream for him to fuck me on this boulder, but I stretched my head up with Fae speed and thrust my tongue to meet with his. My hand searched for his, then trailed it to my breasts. He groaned loudly into me. My chest rattled and his hands kneaded through the tough material of my armor. Hell, this armor was not made for moments like this. I wanted him to rip it off with his teeth, but then I'd have to explain what animal attacked me. And by animal, I meant Rune.

Frustrated with how little I could feel through the hard material, I guided Rune's hand down underneath my waistband.

"Sapphira." My mate's pained groan elicited a plea from my lips. His fingers took over my lead as I kept my hand on his to feel his capable hands caressing my wet slit.

"Rune," I breathed. Slowly, he slipped a finger into me and we moaned into each other's opened mouths.

"Oh, please!" I cried out as low as I could while he slid in and out at an increasing pace. He curled his finger at the right spot while pressing his thumb against my clit. He snarled against my lips and my leg tightened around his waist. His mouth kissed my neck, Fae canines scraping against the sensitive flesh.

"My mate." His lips found mine again with a punishing kiss, like his claim could become a brand on my skin. He was in my body, in my mind, and in my very soul.

"My mate," I whimpered as I tasted blood from our feral clashing of tongue and teeth. My breath hitched as my whole body tensed. That sweet release dangled before me and Rune knew it. He added another finger and the fullness stretched me in a painfully glorious rapture. I gripped him so hard the sound of material ripping mingled with the river beside us. My hand released his shoulder and pulled his head even closer as euphoria crashed into me. I screamed as softly as I could into his mouth and he hungrily swallowed every sound. From my toes to my fingertips, every nerve in my body radiated sweet pleasure in continuous waves.

His fingers slowed their delightful possession of my body and I twitched from the sensitive flesh between my legs. I peered up to see Rune watching me. "I'm not needy anymore," I purred and he smirked.

"Glad I could be of service."

My mate's length still lay hard as a rock against my hip. He leaned down to press a sweet kiss to my swollen and possible bleeding lip.

"Now, it's my Prince's turn," I mumbled, as I palmed that needy member, drawing a growl from my mate's lips.

Chapter Twenty - Six

Tor

Something changed between the fearless leaders of our group two days ago. We'd been traveling without any turbulence, and it made the heated glances between Rune and Sapphira too obvious. They moved as if they were one person, two halves of a whole.

I wanted to feel happy that they figured their shit out and came together. I wasn't angry or sad. I just didn't know where to go in my life now. Should I stay in Crysia and support my brother and my friend? Should I go home and rule as my father wanted me to? Was there still a kingdom to rule? I scoffed at the thought. My father would banish me for life once he found out that Rune is with the princess instead of me. When I thought the princess was in the onyx, I knew I had a destiny that waited once she was released. Was I the model prince waiting for his beloved? No.

I loved Sapphira, but it wasn't the type of love that she and Rune shared. I wanted to protect her, keep her safe, and be somebody to her. However, if I were honest, the princess had too much passion in her than I could handle. She was a warrior inside, and needed someone strong-willed like her. I'd been the safe choice, the ember to her flame. Rune poured accelerants on her fire.

"Look, I know we don't exactly get along, but I can't keep looking at your depressing face. Do you need to talk it out?" Nyx sat beside me on a log as the others slept. It was our night to watch over camp, and I'd been grateful for the alone time. I remained silent as I glanced at her suspiciously. Her long, lavender hair was tied into a ponytail on top her head, and dirt was smudged on her cheek. She looked normal for a change instead of a pompous princess with a big mouth.

"Fine. I need to talk, so I'll start." Her hands rubbed her knees nervously, then she deeply inhaled and exhaled. Was she really going to try and have a conversation with me?

"I'm so out of my depth here. I'm not a skilled warrior or a spy or have a whole library stuffed into my head. Besides helping Sapphira with her magic, which she seems to be getting better at every day, I feel like I have no purpose." Nyx turned her face to the side, away from my shocked stare. She really just opened up to me, and venom didn't spew from her lips.

"I'd been in that tomb for twenty years, and now I don't know where I fit in." She sighed, and my hand reached out to grasp hers. Realizing what I did, I tried to snatch my hand back but her fingers gripped mine harder.

"Please." She shifted her head, and her pleading eyes had my hand relaxing in hers. My natural instinct was to comfort, to make a situation better with humor or understanding. But this was Nyx holding my hand.

"I get it."

I glanced at the tents where Rune and Sapphira slept separately.

"I'm sorry. I know it isn't easy to watch them together." Nyx's thumb rubbed the top of my hand, and a warmth followed the motion, like sitting by the fire. That warmth spread, and I felt calm. I looked at her hand and realized she pushed a little bit of her soothing magic into me. Normally I would have freaked, but tonight I'd accept any help to relax my mind.

"Why are you opening up to me?" Having her sit with me, holding my hand, and soothing me wasn't uncomfortable, but it seemed unnatural for her to be so . . . vulnerable.

"I'm tired of feeling alone. You look very alone, and I thought maybe we could be nicer to each other. Might make us feel a little less alone."

Her admission hit me chest like an arrow. Was I lonely? I'd never felt that way before. I'd always been surrounded by people who were interested in me, who valued me. I knew that this group cared for me, but it was different. Could I trust Nyx? I looked into her face for any hints of a lie. I may not have my powers of truth, but I could still sense it if I really tried. After a moment of staring into her purple eyes, I swear I saw her burning soul exposed in their depths.

"I don't know where I fit in, either." I finally voiced it aloud. Maybe Nyx would use this information to tease me later, but I was tired of pretending.

"You're Prince Torin. You have many things going for you," she said with a sad smile, and I shook my head.

"Yeah, Prince Torin who can't go home, who lost the girl he cared for, and has no real purpose anymore." The tormented thoughts came forth, and the weight I'd placed on my shoulders slightly lessened.

"That's bullshit and you know it."

I stared at her with wide eyes. I finally opened up and she called it bullshit. "How so?" I ripped my hand away from hers, and she frowned.

"You have all the opportunities you could ever want. You're strong, funny, handsome, and one of the best hunters in all the kingdoms I know. You know how to fight, and any woman would be dying to be with you. That particular one just happened to be part of something greater than either of us can understand."

My jaw slacked, and my chest burned like she'd splayed me open. How could this woman who sneered at me the majority of the time with her nose held high in my presence utter such positive words about me?

"Might want to watch your tongue, Nyx. Or I may start to think you like me," I joked to cover up the hope she had blossoming in my mind. She forced a laugh, and flipped her hair to the side, her gaze looking anywhere but me.

"Yeah, good thing you don't have your powers yet or we'd both know that was a lie. I'm just feeling lonely."

I saw the lie in her words and wanted to laugh. I don't know when it happened, or why I never noticed. She had put on a mean face every time she had come near me. Maybe it was all to mask the way she really felt.

"Right," I said. She turned her head farther away from my eyes, but I still saw the blush on her cheeks.

"So I was thinking, maybe we should work on your fighting skills. Rune would be too harsh, and Emrys would probably screw with you the whole time. I could teach you." I extended an invisible olive branch between us, and she faced me with a sparkle in her eyes.

"I'd like that. I think knowing how to fight would make me feel like I had something to bring to the table should we find ourselves in a battle."

She had more to offer than she thought she did. She was devoted, beautiful, and sharp-tongued. I also noticed the small amethyst gems she sprinkled around every camp we'd made to deter any intruders from entering. Hopefully learning some basic defensive and offensive maneuvers would build her confidence back up.

"Great. We'll uh . . . start tomorrow."

And just like that there was a small alliance between us.

Chapter Twenty - Seven

Rune

"This is ridiculous. Just give him the pot!" Sapphira hollered, and I growled but relented. The pond scum we'd ran into hoarded household items in his slimy green and brown folds. Ryan, it called himself. He said he had heard the name from the human realm and liked it.

Ryan looked like a mud monster with a big grin, teeth made of wood, and happy algae-green eyes. Our group had been discussing what path to take to Rainfalls Deep when Ryan had sludged onto the bank of the pond. The creatures gave him space but continued to drink the water on either side of him. He was clearly not a threat, but I'd rather deal with a dangerous creature than an annoying one.

I grabbed the pot from the bag on Nyx's horse and held it out for Ryan to take. Dris's map was outdated, and a completely new river and forest had erected. We were lost, and the only way to get out of this forsaken place was our muddy friend.

"Yes! I prevailed!" Ryan's three fat fingers grasped the pot and covered my hand with thick mud that smelled

"Look, kid . . ." I shifted in his direction, ready to say something to break the uncomfortable silence, but then he hugged me.

I winced, and his grip tightened.

"Thanks for looking out for me, Rune." He released me and took a few steps back. Too many emotions swirled in me and I ached to disappear into the woods to sort through them. This group, this trip was changing me, and I wasn't sure how I felt about it. Sapphira had chosen me, and the others looked to me to lead and protect them. No one feared me, not even Tor, who I assumed hated me and always would with Sapphira as my mate. Confused, and unsure how to feel, I finished readying our beast, then we swiftly got back on trail by following the toadstools.

Chapter Twenty- Eight

Sapphira

Rune decided we needed to rest for the night at one of the ruins on the edge of Rainfall's Deep. There was a pool in the river nearby that fed into a waterfall then disappeared into the darkness at the edge of the gorge. In my memories, the bridge over the thirty-foot-wide and two-mile-long chasm was made of marble with vines weaving between the delicately carved banisters. The pure white temple could be seen from the sky and at one time had beckoned all the artists on the continent. They swore that at night, a creature from the deep would come to them and bless them with inspiration.

However, the past twenty years had not been kind to the bridge or temple. Dirt- and grime-covered posts were all that was left of it. A frightening rope bridge with missing wood steps was tied on the old bridge's columns. The temple was more of a yellow-and-brown color with vines and trees growing through it. No people or artisans were in sight. It was disappointing in the lack of people we had encountered. Verin must have done more than poison the Heart Tree. The Fae could make do without magic, which led me to believe he led his army through here without my mother knowing. My heart ached with the thought of him slaughtering innocent people.

"Food's done!" Nyx announced.

"Good, I'm starving." Emrys sat beside Dris, who stared at the fire where Nyx stirred the soup she had made to warm us up. Emrys and Dris had been nicer to each other, and when I tried to approach the subject, Dris would blurt out a random fact about something she knew. Like pteronophobia is the fear of being tickled by feathers. Or that snakes can predict earthquakes.

She was obviously not comfortable with whatever their relationship was yet. Our group dynamics were slowly changing into that of a family. Even Tor and Rune weren't acting like they wanted to punch each other, which I had been worried about as Rune and I became closer.

Dris had once told me she thought Rune was hard and prickly on the outside, and soft on the inside to those he trusts. She sort of figured him out. He was growly and an asshole at times. But he was also romantic and affectionate toward me, like those soft touches against my skin while we sat by the fire at night. Or the looks of awe he'd give me while we traveled through the woods.

He'd even offered to assist me with practicing magic and fighting skills with Nyx. All of our crew joined in on the training. In a shocking surprise to me, Nyx and Tor had come to a truce. He had been teaching her to fight and their quips weren't as sharp.

I liked how close we were becoming and didn't want it to end.

After dinner, we decided it was time to wash off in the pool, girls to one side and boys to the other. It would have been easy if it weren't for two guys who thought they were funny and pretended to be a monster under the water while we weren't looking. Emrys and Tor both wound up with bloody noses and the stare of angry women all night.

It was my turn to stay awake and this time Emrys stayed up with me. We wanted to rotate and while I loved spending alone time with Rune, we were a distraction to each other. We both knew it and agreed that we wouldn't be on watch at the same time too often.

The air was cold, but a warm breeze shifted from the chasm that kept our camp a few degrees higher. I appreciated it as I sat near the fire and fiddled with my mystery box. I still couldn't open it and I'd tried everything I could think of, including magic. That twenty-year-old seal wouldn't budge.

The fire crackled, and I sighed into the blanket Rune had wrapped around me earlier. He wasn't the type of mate to place me in a bubble to keep me safe from the world. However, he would protect me and stand by my side, letting me fight my own battles. My spirit wouldn't do well being caged or pushed to the sidelines.

"Having issues there?"

I jumped from Emrys's voice breaking through the nighttime silence. "How do you move so quietly!" I whisper-yelled and he grinned as he sat down beside me, glancing at my box. "Yeah. I left this for myself on the top

144

of the palace before I took out my core. But weather and time has damaged the seal, and I can't open it." I lifted the box and peered at the seal again, looking for some clue to breaking it.

"Do you know what's inside?" he asked curiously. His hands lifted and his fingers curled for me to place the box in his hands.

"Nope. It's a mystery box," I admitted as I handed it over.

"Nothing is a mystery around me. I'm kind of offended you didn't ask me to open it." Emrys looked at the box with expert eyes, and I laughed, realizing he had a point. As long as the contents of the box weren't embarrassing, I should have asked him for help days ago. He could get into and out of anything.

He produced a small black pouch from one of his pant pockets and grasped two small metal sticks. He prodded the seal with the devices and pulled his pierced lip between his teeth as he concentrated. Two minutes later, the box hissed and opened. I couldn't believe it!

"It's tough excelling at everything. You may call me Emrys the Magnificent now." Emrys handed me the unsealed box and my shaky hands grasped onto the edges.

"I'm almost afraid to look inside," I breathed. Emrys patted me on the back, assuring me he'd be here with me . . . I wasn't alone.

Slowly, I lifted the lid. It creaked, and I had to pull a little harder than I would have thought but a familiar scent wafted up from the inside. We both peered into the velvet-covered insides with caution.

A bag with tiny diamonds peeked through the top, along with a Sapphira ring, a tiny green bottle with a potent scent leaking from the corked top, and a folded sheet of paper.

"Interesting collection, Princess," my friend commented and watched as I pulled the paper out to read its contents. Maybe it was a note from my mother or Celestine. Maybe I wrote myself a letter to read once I returned. I didn't remember putting these items in here.

"What's it say?"

I flipped the paper over and then back again, analyzing it. All hope I'd harbored about it being a letter of great importance died.

"It's blank."

Chapter Twenty - Nine

Sapphira

Should we attempt to cross the rickety bridge? It was the thought on everybody's mind as we stopped at the ravine.

"It'll add five days to our trip if we go around." Dris added her calculations into the conversation.

"That's if nothing happened in the past twenty years to change the detour." Rune voiced his thoughts as he peered over the edge. There was nothing down there but darkness. At least nothing that we could see. He did have a point, though. We'd learned that the information Dris had wasn't one hundred percent accurate. Going around might take five extra days or it could be twenty.

"Dris's beast could fly us over," Emrys offered and Dris winced.

"She could but only us. You'd have to leave yours bags and pets behind." Rune squashed that glimmer of hope quickly.

Dris frowned, her quick glances to our animals resting near camp made her displeasure for the thoughts clear. I didn't want to leave them, either.

"What about the human realm?" Tor offered with a shrug.

"It's not a bad plan." Rune rubbed his jaw as he considered his brother's alternative.

"What about the Dramens? Surely there will be scouts everywhere since we set their castle on fire." I flung my arms as I made a big plot hole in this idea. Dris quickly lifted her map and scanned it, her lips moving as she talked to herself. Nyx took a step on the roped bridge and it wobbled before the wooden plank splintered. Its old shards fell into the deep chasm.

"I'm all for not crossing the bridge," she said, then stood on the other side of our group, far away from the cliff. If we rode our creatures, we'd be able to move faster than when Tor and I crossed the land. We were only two more days from Crystoria's borders.

"I don't know . . . I need to think on this." I walked to the broken-down temple. I heard chatter after I left but didn't listen to their discussion. Finding a portal to the human realm was the smartest decision. Despite Dramen dangers, I knew we'd make it.

Flashes of the blond Dramen who attacked me burned through my thoughts. I hated that they held power over me like this. I didn't fear the journey, but I feared running into those feral people. They had the resources to hurt my friends. They'd starved and beaten Tor, and the queen would have speared me to death had Rune not jumped in front of it. He almost died protecting me.

Warm hands wrapped around my waist and the scent of waterfall and sandalwood surrounded me. Rune's chin rested on top of my head as I pushed the Dramen's face out of my mind.

"Strategically it's the best plan. Dris found a portal on her map not too far from here." His confident voice led me to nod in agreement. Stories said the artisans would go into the natural forest in the human realm. The humans called them hippies, but they were just Fae who loved nature and the arts. I sighed, knowing that we had to go to the human realm, a place I wanted to avoid.

"Yeah, I know. We need to pack up camp and get all weapons ready just in case." I tried to push out of Rune's hold, but his arms were like steel against me.

"I sense your unease." He lifted his head to kiss mine.

"The portal we need to go through will put us in the Southern Dramens' territory. The worst of them all, and I just don't want anything to happen to our friends. Or you. I just . . ." I panicked as the words rushed from my mind through my mouth. I wiggled to be free of Rune. The feeling of being contained was too much right now. He released me but as I spun around to continue my wallowing, he stepped closer and his calloused hands cupped my jaw softly.

"You are the most powerful Fae in all the realms. There is nothing they can do to hurt you now." His soothing reminder warmed my chest, but my mind still raced.

"But they can hurt you and everyone I love." Tears stung at my eyelids. I hated that those bastards scared me so much.

"I see. You're not afraid of those humans. You just wanted me to follow you over here so you can admit that you love me without the others hearing." He teased me to lighten my thoughts, and I groaned. Wrong time for nice Rune to show his stupid smirking face. I needed the angry, growling protector Rune. The werewolf side of him to break free and eat any Dramens we encountered.

"You're ridiculous!" I threw my hands in the air, exasperated from his joking mood.

"I agree it's ridiculous to love a cursed prince with a werewolf rattling inside him, but here you are, confessing your love to him." He smiled and my thoughts were on his white canines. I loved Rune's smile, a gift that he rarely shared with anyone. He knew what he was doing, pushing aside his hard shell to distract me from following my thoughts down a deeper ravine than Rainfall's Deep. There was always a chance that something bad could happen, but something right could happen, too. Both were plausible. We needed to be aware of the danger and hope for the best outcomes. I shook my head, and Rune leaned down to kiss me victoriously.

"It's not ridiculous to love a cursed prince with a werewolf inside him, and since you are not cursed, when you find one let me know so I can confess my undying love for him." I pursed my lips to keep from laughing but he could see it in my eyes.

"Only you." He shook his head, one of his hands ran through his black hair and I reached up to do the same.

"Only you," I repeated but with more tenderness in my tone. This jackass was my mate for life, and I'd protect him at all costs.

"I choose you, Sapphira. Human, Fae, mate, or not. I choose us in this life and the next." He held out his hand and opened it before me. Resting in his palm, next to a tiny star-shaped scar was the tiger's eye ring I'd been keeping in my bra since Nyx gave them to me.

"Rune," I gasped, then eyed him suspiciously.

"How did you?" I asked, then my cheeks heated as I remembered when he caught me by surprise this morning with his hands and lifted me against a tree, his lips devouring mine. His fingers must have found the jewelry while they teased my breasts. Sneaky Fae. He reached out and placed the ring in my hand.

"When you're ready to choose us, know that I'm giving this ring to you again with the same devotion, loyalty, and love that's burned in my soul since the moment you stabbed me in my damn shoulder." His fingers caressed my cheek, then my lips, and stopped over my beating heart.

"I wanted you to know it's not just jewelry to me. My promises that I'd made in the past still stand with the woman you are now." The right side of his lips tilted up and tears threatened to roll down my cheeks. Over our travels Rune had been softening pieces of the armor around his heart, and I felt honored to be subjected to his growth.

"Why do you have to be so damn sweet right now? It makes you too perfect and I am going to become too obsessed with hearing your words." I covered my tears and grin with my hands, which he pulled away from my face.

"Then I guess I'll have to be sweet to you every day for the rest of our immortal lives." He kissed my hands and I lunged for him. Our bodies fell to the temple and I rained kisses across his face.

"I love you, you sweet, and growling jackass."

He growled as I kissed him on his scars, then his lips.

"And I choose us forever." I smiled against his lips and kissed him over and over.

Until someone coughed, and I remembered our friends were only fifty feet away.

Chapter Thirty

Sapphira

I don't think anyone can get over the feeling of switching realms. The small portal we found was barely big enough to fit us and our creatures. Rune and Emrys had to push Silvio's big bear butt through. I swear that black bear grinned the whole time they grunted and sweat beaded on their brows. My gloriously grumpy mate barked more than five times how tempted he was to leave his friend behind.

Finally we all made it through the shimmering portal and found ourselves in a steamy cave. It was like stepping out of the bath in a fifty-foot-wide space.

"We need to find a way out of here before we have to take off our winter gear." Nyx fanned her face with her hands. She pulled her armor out slightly to circulate some air to her chest. I knew the feeling. Emrys grinned, ready to toss a naughty joke at her but Dris poked him in the side with her pointy finger. Nyx did leave herself open for teasing after that comment.

I wondered where we were in the human realm. All the portals sat in national parks so they wouldn't be destroyed. The royals of the kingdoms would cross the portals on the first day of every year. The parks were closed to the public so they wouldn't be seen. Then they would talk about matters of security. Fae were allowed to travel to the realm as long as they didn't expose themselves or try to conquer the lands. My mother and the queen of Crystoria were strong-handed and did not tolerate any rebel Fae trying to enslave the humans.

However, humans were not allowed to come to our world. I always thought it would have been a good thing, but our values were too different. The Fae leaders of the world decided in unity that we needed to keep humans out of our realm. They trashed their earth, and they were not safe in our world. Monsters from their nightmares roamed our woods, and while they had guns, those violent machines would never take down a creature like an ogre with its skin like an alligator.

"This path should lead to an exit." Dris took the lead, and her wolfawk followed. We walked up a stony walkway and the higher up we went, the cooler the air became.

"Shit. Emrys!" The goat Fae weaseled his way to the front where Dris was. Metal bars blocked our path out. Dris shook the bars twice, but they didn't budge. Emrys jumped into action with his picks.

"The lock is melted shut. It'll take me a few minutes."

A tingle grew beneath my skin. I needed to answer a burning question I'd thought all the way to the portal.

"Stand back, everybody. It's time to see if magic works here." Our crew split so I could walk to the metal gate and I pressed my hand to it. Metal was made from the earth, so I should be able to move it with Rune's power.

"Deep breaths, Sapphira," Nyx coaxed me, and I imagined the metal bending to my will. I heard a creak and smiled. But when I opened my eyes, nothing had changed. In my anger, I made the ground beneath the gate launch upward and the metal contorted to the rock spikes. I pulled the earth back into the ground and the metal bars fell out of our way.

"And people say I have anger problems," Rune mumbled.

"Ah, fresh air." Dris breathed in the crisp air as we stepped into the bare woods. To the left of us were pools with steam wafting off the water—a hot spring. I mentally ran through the national parks in my head that Dris had taught me.

"This must be the Hot Springs National Park!" Dris squealed and looked around, grinning in delight.

"Before we continue, who has been to the human realm before? Besides our trip to the Iron city?" I asked and Tor raised his hand despite all of us knowing he'd been on the continent with me. Nyx raised her hand next.

"I've been a few times. The fashion is spectacular."

"I've been, but I was banned from the main portals after a misunderstanding with their president." Emrys chewed on his pierced lip and I eyed him suspiciously. I'd need to hear this story at a later time.

"Besides our trip to the Iron City, never had the honor." Dris walked to the closest tree and touched the bark, then inspected her fingers. She frowned, then walked back to where we stood. In the Fae realm you could almost hear nature. Everything was connected. Here, even though humans haven't been terrorizing the forests for a long time, the network between life forces seemed disjointed.

"I've been," Rune announced, and I wondered when he came to this realm before. Honestly besides Dris you could hear it in the other's speech. Fae had adopted many words of the human language over the centuries like fuck. That was not a Fae word at all, but I enjoyed using it.

"According to Dris's map, we should only be about a two-day ride from Crystoria. Their portal will be guarded, but we will be allowed in. In the meantime, watch out for Dramens. I have a feeling they will be everywhere searching for us since we ravaged their city." I mounted Cara, who purred as I stroked her long, furry neck. The catagaro and I had grown closer, and I found myself talking to her more as a friend than a pet. She liked fish, and birds were her favorite meal, and she liked to sleep on the large branches of trees.

"Keep your weapons ready and eyes open." Rune slung his muscular leg over Silvio's back and the bear wiggled to get comfortable with his rider. Emrys had been alternating rides so one creature wouldn't tire having to carry another person every day. Today was Tor's unicorn's turb to share the load. Yesterday, I'd barely been able to hold in my laughter when it was Rune's turn to share with him. My mate's face was pinched in frustration the whole way, while Emrys fought the urge to screw with him.

Winter had taken over the lands and dusts of snow covered the ground. Dris took the lead with Rune as they navigated our way toward Crystoria. Although this time crossing the continent was better than the last where it was more about survival, the desires were the same. I wanted to sleep in a bed and take a hot bath. My muscles ached from so much riding, plus practicing with my powers and fighting techniques.

Cara's neck hairs rose, and a rattling sound vibrated beneath me. Silvio's fur did the same and the bear stopped walking.

"They sense a threat." Rune touched Silvio's neck, his attention darting around the woods. Because winter left the trees bare, there wasn't much to cover us from being spotted, especially when we stood out as riders on such strange beasts.

"I don't see anything," Tor said and Emrys nodded, his hands going to his sword.

"Pick up the pace," Rune demanded and we nudged our rides to move faster.

POW.

A gunshot echoed and I fearfully analyzed my friends to see if someone had been shot.

"Go! GO!" Rune bellowed and our beasts took off at full speed as Dramens yelled. More shots were fired around us while we raced for our lives.

157

Chapter Thirty - One

Nyx

"Nyx, stay close!" Tor snapped at me. Loud bangs of gunfire rang through the air around us and my heart beat as fast as Persephone's hooves galloped. I pulled the sword from the holster at my back and grasped it tightly. A nagging feeling in my head suggested I steer my horse to the right, and just as I did a bullet flew past where I'd been.

I screamed from the sheer terror of being shot at, and I pleaded with Persephone to guide us onward. I knew if I panicked, the others would get distracted, but my power to remain calm wasn't working.

"It's OK, Nyx. We're going to be OK." Sapphira slowed her catagaro to run beside me and talk me down.

"Just breathe, and remember your training." Sapphira reached out a hand and touched my shoulder. Warmth spread throughout me and the constricting grip fear had on my chest. She was pushing my own calming powers into me.

"Better?" she asked, and I nodded. I had been working with them on techniques for fighting. I could do this. Intuition was a familiar guide in the well of my powers. I could use it as a strength in this battle.

The clopping of horses reverberated from behind us, and I turned to see ten men with dirt on their faces. They wore leather and animal pelts over their body. I had a gift of reading people, and they looked at us like food, purely for their pleasure. Sapphira had been right when she had described these monsters. They were definitely not human.

"I think they were waiting for us. But how would they know we would show up here?" Emrys shouted and I had been thinking the same thing. Sapphira said they would be looking for us but the more I looked around, the more men I saw. There was an army here, and we had walked right into their trap.

"Could have been Verin," Dris said as her wolfawk leaped over a fallen tree.

"I don't think so. He wouldn't have let us get this far," Tor responded.

I heard the snap of a bowstring from his direction. I glanced at him to see that he and Emrys had switched places on the horse. Emrys held the reins and Tor's torso was twisted shooting arrows at the Dramens behind us.

"Show-off," I murmured and Tor grinned slightly. Ever since that night we had talked, things have been different. He teased me but I didn't feel like he did it because he was a jerk. It was his way of comforting us, bringing light to the dark.

"Shit!" Rune cursed, and I remembered we were being shot at. This was not a good time to stare at Tor's lips or remember our newfound friendship.

My hands shook as fifty angry Dramens stood in front of the gates out of the park with guns pointed at us.

Sapphira lifted her hands and a wall of fire grew between us. "I can't do this forever." She focused on the wall, and I knew what she would say next.

"There's only fifty. We are faster, stronger, and smarter than they are. I vote we fight and haul ass out of here."

Emrys jumped off the black unicorn and produced two swords, one for each hand. The hollers from the Dramens behind us were closing in. We'd be surrounded if we didn't do something quickly. I looked at Persephone and patted her head. I wasn't ready to lose my horse to these monsters so I swung my body over her side.

"Go, Persephone. You can find me after but you run away from here." I stared into her green eyes, then smacked her backside as hard as I could. She ran, and I held my sword a little tighter. "I'm going to fight."

"Me too." Tor smacked the side of his horse and Mars took off. Bullets would surely kill our animals, and I wasn't willing to risk that right now. We could move faster, even without powers. Rune, Sapphira, and Dris all told their animals to go, and the sounds of gunfire spooked them into running away. They could find us if they wanted, and I hoped they would come back after this fight ended.

"I can't hold it much longer. Get ready." Sweat coated Sapphira's face.

"Their formation seems to be stationed around one man in the middle. He's probably their superior." Dris's quick observational skills were invaluable. She readied her white bow and Emrys walked up to stand beside her. They looked into each other's eyes with longing of saying words they wished they'd said. I had confidence we'd win this fight, but I knew there was also a chance someone could get hurt

"I love you guys," I said, before digging my boot into the dirt and pushing off toward the army. I had feared where I stood in this group, but now, I knew my place. I would fight for my princess and help us win. The others were at my side in a heartbeat.

Sapphira's firewall came down as we reached its borders and saw the wide-eyed look of the Dramens. Two arrows protruded from the man in the middle and I glanced at Tor with that thankful grin.

I rammed my sword into the first Dramen I saw and moved faster than ever on light feet. Blood splattered against my skin and lavender hair as I sliced my way through the army.

Grunts and the sound of metal hitting swords bounced off the trees.

"I'm gonna fuck this one raw," a Dramen growled from my right, and I turned just in time to see him pointing a handgun at me. His pulled the trigger at the same time I lunged to the side, my body smashing into another

Dramen. I sliced quickly and the bloody arm of the man with the handgun flew through the air.

I smiled, as confidence radiated from within. I was really doing this . . . fighting and helping. I quickly glanced to see the rest of our group. Rune's face was covered in blood but he had that glint in his eyes like he was at home on this small battlefield. Tor was on top of the brick gate firing arrow after arrow into the crowd. Emrys and Dris were like the wind, carving through the crowd, dodging bullets as they moved. I could see the end of the crowd, to where we could get away. All we needed to do was get enough space from the Dramens and our Fae speed would save us.

Pain burned through my leg, and I found a window of time to glance where the pain was coming from. Blood soaked my pants, and I groaned.

"King said your group was coming. Glad I was the one to kill you. Now I can get the bounty."

Someone gripped my ponytail hard and jerked me off my feet. I kicked and flung my sword in the man's direction but another Dramen grabbed my arm. I screamed as they yanked me like a doll, then suddenly their hands released me and I scrambled two feet away. The three men that had grabbed me laid on the ground with arrows sticking out of their eye sockets. I tried to find my friends, but on the ground, I couldn't see them.

"Sapphira!" I called out, blood gushing from my leg. I knew I was in trouble.

"Tor!" I screamed, and a Dramen noticed me among the dead bodies of his comrades. Shit.

Then a large sandy-colored creature leaped onto him, and its massive fangs dug deep into his neck.

"Cara!" I sobbed as Sapphira's catagaro lunged for another Dramen, and then another. A roar came from my right and Rune's bear Silvio had joined the fight. He smashed his huge paw against the head of a soldier and it came clean off to roll on the grass. Soon Tor's unicorn and Dris's wolfawk joined the fight. We would make it out of here.

Well . . . at least they would. I needed to stop this bleeding before I passed out. A soft neigh echoed behind me, and Persephone nudged me with her head. I grasped onto her antlers to steady me as I stood. She lowered herself to the ground and I stepped with my good leg into the stirrup to hoist myself up, but I was losing strength. My muscles shook as I exerted more power than they had to give.

"I got you." Tor's hand wrapped around my waist and helped me onto Persephone. I gripped her reins and swayed. A large body pressed against my back and I looked to see Tor had climbed on, too.

"I will take those." He lightly took the reins just in time. My vision blurred and I leaned against his chest before succumbing to the blood loss.

Chapter Thirty - Two
Rune

"Get her out of here!" I barked at Tor, who held an unconscious and bleeding Nyx on her horse. He nodded, and they galloped down the street.

"Emrys, you take Mars. It's time we get out of here." He wiped the blood from his brow before running to the unicorn. He was gone in an instant, and Dris followed.

Silvio roared beside me and I climbed up as my eyes searched for Sapphira. She'd been tired from using her powers but every glimpse I saw of her she was using her training and winning. Cara and the other animals had shown up and finished the remaining Dramens.

"Sapphira, let's go." She sat on top of her catagaro twenty feet from me ready to ride, but her eyes were on the woods behind us. A group of Dramens were running toward us, some with guns firing in our direction and some held metal weapons in their hands.

"Sapphira, we need to go." I growled. We had our opening, and the opportunity to escape. Why was she frozen? Cara hissed at the group but didn't move.

"He's there," she whispered in a trembling voice.

Surely Verin wouldn't be here, but I couldn't put anything past him. He wanted Sapphira dead at all costs. I walked Silvio over to her.

"The Dramen that killed . . . that killed Mariam and touched . . ." Her lip wobbled and I wished I could turn into my werewolf side. For I second, I thought of asking Sapphira to help me change over. A Dramen with blond hair and a blond beard stepped onto the snow-dusted road.

"Pretty girl, pretty girl." He taunted my mate and I snarled. "She'll be taken care of after you are dead."

A bloody rage settled over my vision as I docked an arrow in my bow within seconds.

"Wait!" Sapphira threw a hand in front of my face and my hands held the arrow against the string instead of releasing.

"Got you in control, I see," he said, continuing to disrespect my princess.

"She's probably got a magical pussy, like that bitch-mom of hers. She screamed at first but after the first two men were done, she moaned for more." He took a step closer and my aim narrowed at his Adam's apple. He would drown in his own blood. A few of his men laughed and made vulgar gestures with their hands. I'd been born into battle. It's where I felt the most familiar. Killing the twenty men standing before us would be over before it started. I'm glad I didn't have my powers, so I'd bask in doing it with my hands.

"Rune." Sapphira's trembling voice transformed into confidence.

"He is mine. You can have the rest." She glanced at me before her narrowed gaze shifted to the leader who raped Mariam and touched her.

Sapphira hopped off Cara and walked toward the Dramen without a weapon in her hands. She could use any of her powers and kill them all in seconds. But my mate had a lust to dispose of the murderer who had wronged her with her own hands.

My warrior princess.

"Let's play." The Dramen lifted a hunting knife and licked the edge.

"She's mine first. You boys can fuck the pieces once I'm done."

Fuck this. I was done with their disgraceful and dirty faces. I fired at a Dramen with a large gun, then leaped off Silvio. I darted to the men just as the lead Dramen swiped his knife at Sapphira. She dodged him and sent her fist flying straight into his bearded jaw.

Tor was right about one thing he had said to me. I was a legend on the battlefield, and these fuckers were about to find out why. Three assholes lunged for me at the same time and I sidestepped them. Their bulky bodies collided in a mixture of grunts. I heard the woosh of an axe coming my way and spun around to kick the arm of the

Dramen. The axe flew up, and I grabbed the hilt and whirled it straight across his muddy neck.

I glanced at my woman with a satisfied smirk and saw the Dramen leader sweat and spit blood to the ground. I didn't fear her safety. I knew she could kill them all right now with any of the powers in her arsenal. She pushed her curly brown hair away from her eyes and her gaze found mine. Her smirk matched mine, and I craved my warrior princess, my match in every way. That old meddling seer was right. Sapphira was my fire and my balm. Only my mate would smirk on a field of battle. The wolf within howled for her, and I swear he was close to coming out just to claim her. We'd defy the moon and declare her the true master of our heart and soul. I was done playing with these scums. I wanted to claim my mate's lips.

I slowly pulled my black sword from the scabbard. I sliced with one hand and swung the dead Dramen's axe with the other. Blood splatted against my face as I stabbed my blade through the bearded skull of the last man.

My gaze found Sapphira as she toyed with the man who murdered her guardian and violated her.

I snarled low and savagely at the male. Sapphira withdrew one of her hatchets and brought it down on his hands. Four fingers tumbled into the grass. The Dramen wailed and grasped at his bleeding nubs.

"My moon." I walked to her and lifted a hand to caress her cheek. Blood smeared against her beautiful brown skin. I'd never felt more secure that this perfect woman was meant for me than I did now.

"You bitch." The Dramen foamed at the mouth and lunged for her. Without taking her eyes off of me, she held a delicate hand toward him and flames engulfed his body. It spread to the dead around us, and I leaned down to kiss my mate as her fire burned brightly.

Chapter Thirty - Three

Sapphira

When he growled against my lips, I wanted him right there in that field of fiery blood and death. Only my mate would look at me after the fighting I'd done and see me—the true Sapphira. We were a warrior prince and princess, together in arms against evil.

The hatchet that had been in my other hand fell to the grass, and I reached up to run my fingers through his hair.

"Sapphira." He groaned and I pulled his head closer.

"I swear when we get to Crystoria, you're mine." My body and mind were in a battle high where I couldn't think of anything but his body clashing with mine. But he broke through my lust-driven haze.

"We have to check on the others," my mate reminded me as I remembered.

Fuck! Nyx had passed out! We separated and ran to our animals, who waited patiently for us. I knew Nyx wouldn't have gone far and would wait for us. We made it about a mile away from the hot springs little town before we saw a familiar face.

"Princess." Emrys jumped out from beside a large house with leafless vines wrapped around the four columns on the front.

"How is everyone?" I demanded, as we unmounted. The creatures walked to a big garage with the other animals that were drinking from a trough of water.

"Tor and Dris have a few bruises and minor cuts. I'm good, but Nyx got shot in the leg. She lost a lot of blood. Dris bandaged her up and used some plant to protect it from infection." Emrys led the way through the abandoned home, where portraits of a happy family stared at us while we walked through the hallway.

"Sapphira, Rune. I'm so glad you guys are OK. We didn't see you behind us but I knew you'd be here shortly, and you're covered in a lot more blood and you smell like fire, and I was just so worried," Dris rambled, and I pulled her in for a hug.

She was scared, but I was so proud of her for fighting. Tears grew in her big owl eyes, and I smiled. I walked past her to the bed where Nyx laid peacefully. She was still unconscious and my stomach dropped when the flashbacks of her in that onyx tomb barreled into my mind.

"We need to get her to Crystoria." Tor's voice was low and assertive.

"I agree." I nodded.

Dris talked with Rune about the fastest way to get there. Everyone awake agreed to ride through the night without rest. She needed the healer's touch and that wasn't something any of us could do. Dris knew some things from her books, but it wasn't enough.

"She can ride with me," I offered and pushed the hair out of her face.

"She's riding with me," Tor growled and my eyebrows shot up. He had been acting like Nyx's guard dog ever since we walked into the room, which seemed completely out of character for him.

"Tor are you OK?"

"I'm fine. She's just riding with me." His challenging stare dared me to say no. Rune placed a comforting hand on my shoulder, and I blinked up at him. Something weird was going on, but all I could think about was getting to Crystoria.

"Let's go. Grab anything we can use from the house and hurry."

Tor wrapped Nyx tenderly in a blanket and carried her down the hall to his mount.

"That was odd," I said to myself, vowing to dissect what happened later. For now, I searched for anything useful in the house, but the house had already been raided. Anything worth using was either gone or expired. I was the last to come out of the house and I climbed onto Cara immediately.

Tor spurred Mars to go and Emrys rode Persephone behind him. Dris was next, then Rune and me. We pushed our beast until their breaths grew too labored. We gave them water, food, and a short rest before racing onward. We'd get a short-lived break before searching for the Heart Tree. The snow grew heavier as we headed into the rolling mountains where the portal to Crystoria would be. Riding through the freezing night would be difficult but luckily our animals and Dris could see in the darkness. She'd continue to lead while we bundled up and hoped we'd found the portal before the weather worsened. The time passed as we rode. No one talked or even smiled, driven by the common goal to help Nyx.

I glanced at Tor and caught him whispering to Nyx's sleeping face a few times. They'd grown closer over the past few days. Nyx had mentioned that they found common ground. Were they becoming something more than friendly? I hoped so. Tor deserved someone who made him happy and same with Nyx. However, I had trouble seeing them as a couple after the many memories of them spatting at each other. He thought she was a spoiled princess and she thought him to be an arrogant jerk. I'm fairly sure even Rune didn't vex her as much as Tor had in the past.

Soon the night had transformed into morning and according to Dris, we were close. We needed to keep our eyes open for a large yellow tree with intricately carved doors like the Crysia's main portal. There should be guards stationed around it wearing golden armor. Crysia's armor was silver while Verin's was black and red.

We reached the Great Smokey Mountain National Park sign among the bare trees and looked around for our salvation. I briefly remembered passing by here and hadn't remembered the portal to the Fae realm.

"If I'm reading our map right, we should be close." Dris slowed her wolfawk and analyzed the woods. The rest of us slowed alongside her and looked for the yellow tree.

Suddenly, Rune shifted in his saddle with his bow drawn and an arrow docked. One breath passed and the arrow was soaring through the air into the woods at our right. A grunt echoed from the direction of his shot, then a man fell from a tree.

"Dramen scout. We need to keep moving," Rune explained and gestured for us to keep moving.

"Sapphira." A weak voice came from the blanket wrapped Nyx leaning against Tor.

"I'm here." I steered Cara to them and looked at her with a smile. She was still alive, but her face looked so pale. Her normally luscious lavender hair appeared to have lost some of its shine. She tried to smile then closed her eyes and drifted back into an unconscious state.

Panic filled my chest, and I nudged Cara onward. We needed to find that tree before Dramens found us.

Chapter Thirty - Four

Sapphira

We'd been searching for an hour in this park and had yet to see the tree. Dris even flew above the canopy and looked for it.

"I'm curious if the tree will even have leaves with it being winter." Emrys voiced his thoughts and I wrung the reins within my fists over and over as my insides quivered. Nyx may not have much more time.

"Sorry guys." I apologized right before I yelled into the woods. "Guards of Crystoria! I am Princess Sapphira from Crysia. We need sanctuary!" I called for the guards as well as announced to any enemies in the area where we were. I made a dangerous choice but I was desperate. Rune stared at me like I was insane for giving away our position.

"Cara, run," I told my beast and she dug her paws into the ground and launched us forward. I screamed those same calls for sanctuary again and again. Only the wind brushing against the branches answered my calls. Still, I wasn't giving up. Cara raced through the woods and through a dark tunnel, I yelled at the top of my lungs until I heard it. The sound of hoofs coming from the distance ahead of me. My comrades caught up to where I was and we readied our weapons just in case.

"Please be a Crystorian guard," Dris whispered and I pleaded the same sentiments in my head.

"Princess Sapphira!" A woman called my name and my heart beat rapidly. Shimmers of gold peeked through trees. A guard of Crystoria. We made it! Cara raced toward the woman in armor.

"We've been looking for you. We're so glad you made it." The woman grinned as we came to a stop fifteen feet away from her. Her horse whinnied and stomped the ground seeing our creatures, but the guard reined it in.

"We are in desperate need of a healer. Please take us to the portal now." The guard glanced at my friends curiously.

"Right. This way." She turned her horse around and led us to the portal.

"Hold on, Nyx," I said to my unconscious friend, and we rode as a group behind our new guide.

"My wolf is growling and not the good kind," Rune whispered close to me and my eyebrows pinched together. That didn't seem right.

My eyes narrowed at the guard for any signs she wasn't who she appeared to be. She looked poised and clean, like a soldier should, with no tattoos, piercings, or dirty appearance which would scream Dramen.

"I don't know, Rune." I decided to investigate the werewolf's reaction.

"How is the kingdom holding up these days?" I scooted Cara closer to her horse and opened dialogue between us.

"Good. The queen has been busy," she mused and I nodded.

"Have they constructed those twenty-eight libraries yet? I heard it was put on hold." I asked a completely wild question. Crystoria was known for its one and only great library.

"Not yet. They are still on hold," the woman answered and I thrust my axe against her throat.

"Who are you?" I snarled, and the woman had the gall to laugh.

"You are too gullible."

I hit the hilt of my axe against the back of her head. She collapsed against her horse's neck, as I heard a twig snap thirty yards away. Shit! She had led us straight to the Dramen camp. I was so desperate to find Crystoria that I led us straight to a trap. Another group of Dramen, although smaller, but we needed a healer immediately.

"Tor, take Nyx and keep searching. We'll take care of this," I commanded him and he nodded.

Only before he could move, a hundred arrows fell on the Dramens waiting for us. Their grunts and wails of pain were no trick of the ears. I shifted in my saddle so fast my back cracked, and I saw a glorious sight—ten soldiers in golden armor with their bows raised.

"Princess Sapphira, Queen Dinesiri commanded we find you. One of our guards heard you shouting. We received a letter from Ryka that you traveled to our borders. We are so grateful you have made it safely." A female soldier emerged from the middle of the group, and I sagged against Cara. These were Crystorian soldiers sitting on a variety of magical-looking creatures.

"One of my friends is hurt. She needs a healer immediately. Please."

The woman said to the man on her right, "Rohja, ride to healer Kryo at once and tell him to ready his quarters."

To us, she said, "This way. We are not far from the portal."

We followed them through the woods until we came across a large tree with cherry wood-colored doors. We were so close, but Emrys's thoughts ran true. The leaves were gone in the winter. The tree had become identical to all the others. Two armed guards opened the large double doors, and we walked through. The portal tickled, and I breathed the sweet scent of apples in the air of Crystoria.

Chapter Thirty - Five

Tor

The guards rushed us through the city to the healer's quarters. No one muttered a word about the architecture or the people as we passed, not even Dris. Healer Kryo stood outside the wooden door of his stone quarters. His long black hair swished behind him as he rushed to us.

"What happened?"

"Bullet wound to the thigh. She's lost a lot of blood." I carried her into the building. A padded table was ready for her, and three Fae healers waited to assist their leader when necessary.

"The house we were staying at had some neem oil, so I soaked some on to help prevent any infections until we got here." Dris stood beside me as I laid Nyx down on the table. She looked exactly how she did in the onyx tomb for all those years, and I wanted to shake her to wake up. I'd been so wrong about her. Shame ate at my insides. I needed to make it up to her, apologize. Tell her how amazing and beautiful she was. She wasn't some spoiled princess that played with pretty dresses all day while snubbing her nose at people. She was a princess who wanted to serve another and would willingly fight for her and a higher purpose.

"We will take care of this. Don't worry. She will be all right." Kryo gave me a firm nod and the other healers pushed us toward the door.

"I want to stay with her." The lead healer shook his head.

"Please send word to us when she wakes up," Sapphira said and placed a hand on my shoulder to comfort me. For the first time, her touch did not soothe me. I didn't need her right now. I needed Nyx to wake up and look at me with those purple eyes and call me a jerk.

"Come on. Let's give the healers some room to fix Nyx," Sapphira whispered softly and I shrugged her hand off me, then stormed out the door. If they needed us to give them space, I'd stand outside the building and wait.

"I'm glad she's going to be OK." Dris sighed and leaned against Sapphira, who hugged her. We were all happy except Rune, whose icy stare was aimed at me. Probably didn't like that I shrugged off Sapphira's hand, but fuck it.

"Princess Sapphira," someone called from a group of people walking toward us. Two guards led the front of the group but stopped ten feet away from us.

"Oh, she's not a danger to me. Get out of the way." A female shooed the guards out of our sight and stepped closer. She was tall and had dark-brown skin with shimmering gold tattoos on her forehead, neck, and arms. The tattoo on her head glistened like a crown with a point between her eyebrows. The intricately swirled bands around her neck and upper arm shimmered like magic. Her hair was braided and adorned with gold jewels. But her eyes were not gold, they were smoky gray.

"Queen Dinesiri?" Sapphira stepped away from Dris and bowed.

"Honey bug, is that any way to treat your aunt?" The queen closed the distance between them, her white halter gown flowing as she moved.

"Aunt?" Sapphira croaked as the queen squeezed her tightly. She rocked with the princess in her arms, then took a step back to get a good look at her.

"You look so much like your parents." The queen lifted a finger to wipe away the tears that were cresting over her cheeks.

"You're my—"

"I'm Desmire's younger and smarter sister." Her eyes sparkled with joy.

"My dad. You're my dad's sister . . . and Verin's." Sapphira winced, saying the name aloud.

The queen's voice became solemn. "Lachan was the name he was born with but another side of him always creeped below the surface. An evil side. Ryka sent us a detailed letter with the happenings of Crysia and Verin's identity revealed. Don't worry, my child, he will be brought to justice for his crimes." At that moment the Queen looked like a fearsome Fae. The gold in the queen's tattoos shimmered like flames dancing beneath her skin. She was not one to fuck with.

180

"He will," Sapphira agreed and then the Queen addressed the rest of us.

"You must be the brave friends that journeyed with the princess. I am honored and blessed to have you in my kingdom. If there is anything you all should need, my people are ready to help." She bowed her head in gratitude, and we did the same.

"General Rune, always a blessing to see you, my dear." The queen chuckled and Sapphira stiffened.

"She has that annoying family trait of pissing me off on purpose to ruffle my feathers." Rune leaned down to Sapphira and cooled the jealousy growing within her. I rolled my eyes. Rune never looked at another female with interest after he saw Sapphira. Jealousy was one emotion the princess didn't need to harbor.

"It is quite fun." The queen winked at Sapphira and then greeted each of us. Dris was in awe and could barely speak. The queen vowed to show her the library this evening and I swear the owl Fae swayed a bit. Emrys was granted freedom within the kingdom, making nothing off-limits or taboo, which immediately took away any interest on the spider's part.

"I think you all look very weary and are in need of hospitality. We can continue conversations at dinner tonight. I will have a glorious feast in your honor. And you will also get to meet my wife. She will scream when I tell her you have made it." The queen clapped her hands and gestured for us to follow her to the palace.

181

In the distance, it appeared to have been carved from the mountain with arches and greenery growing on the sides. Stained glass windows brought color to the white stone, giving the place an artistic impression. Crystoria was known for its artsy and brainy side. Crystorians valued intelligence, magic, truth, arts, and science.

"I'm gonna wait here. I'll let you guys know when Nyx wakes up," I said to the group, as they started walking with the queen. Sapphira turned to speak but Rune wrapped his arm around her and pulled her away. He gave me a nod.

I leaned against the healer's stone quarters and pushed at the thoughts of Nyx bleeding on the ground with those three demons' hands on her. Her screams echoed within my brain until darkness claimed me. I breathed in and exhaled through the painful memories. She was going to be OK, and soon I'd tell her how sorry I was that I didn't protect her more.

Chapter Thirty - six

Sapphira

My aunt was an intense woman and yet I enjoyed her company. I shook my head remembering the jealousy I'd had when she looked happy to see Rune. I knew he had lovers, but he was mine now. Only mine.

On our way to the palace, she talked about a few of the times she had played a prank on the general over the years simply because she was a queen and could get away with it. She didn't fear him like many did. She respected him and apparently when she liked you, she played around with you.

"If I'm serious toward you, that means I don't like you. Take it from me, dear. Don't waste your gorgeous smiles on those who aren't worthy."

She bumped shoulders with mine. I hoped I could be a queen like her and my mother one day.

Crystoria was amazing—grand and full of life. People tinkered with inventions or walked around with books five inches away from their face. There wasn't a river winding through the city like in Crysia, but there were a few springs dotted around and a lake behind the palace.

"My lady, your bath is ready." The redheaded servant with mini-brown horns on top of her head bowed and lifted her hands toward the bathroom.

The room was beautiful, carved from different types of stone. There must be many sculptors in Crystoria. A bang on the door startled me and the two servants in the room. I knew that bang and went to open the door, but the quieter brown-haired petite servant got there first.

"Hello General Ru—"

"Get out!" he barked and I swear the poor girl jumped. He stepped inside and searched the room till his heated eyes found me. Instantly I smirked, it seemed my mate had meant his vow earlier. The servants quickly ran out the door, shaking with every step. The door slammed behind them, and we were alone.

Rune and I stared at each other, a challenge dangling in the air between us. Who would lunge first?

"You're going to need to apologize to those girls." I tilted my head and began unclasping my armor slowly. His eyes followed every movement.

"Later," he growled.

I turned my back to him and placed my armor on the dresser closest to me. The submissive gesture would drive the werewolf in him into a frenzy. Rune was instantly at my back, his nose grazing the side of my neck.

"Do you need something, Rune?" My head fell against his shoulder to give him more room to play with.

And what a glorious fire to scorch in. Sapphira exploded around me, and I leaned down to taste her moans. I slammed into her as the waves of her ecstasy crashed into her body again and again. Her fingernails dug into my back and her teeth broke the skin of my lip. I loved my little savage princess. The pain and her clenching warmth had my release barreling into me. I roared and she greedily drank it in. Her nails scratched the length of my back, then gripped my ass closer to her, completely seating myself to the hilt inside her.

Suddenly the bed trembled and started to sink. "Uh, Sapphira?" I laughed and her eyes widened.

"I'm so sorry." She reached her hands toward the ground beside the bed and the bed rose again to its previous height. She was so caught up in her orgasmic bliss that she had accidentally released my earth power and the bed started descending.

"So embarrassing." She covered her face with her hands and I chuckled.

The movement of our laughter shot a tingle up my spine. "Mmm." I moaned at the sight, and Sapphira peeked between her fingers.

"Mine." I moaned again and rolled my hips against her.

"Yours." She flipped me over before I could think. Fae speed was a hell of an advantage. She moved over me and my hands gripped her hips. My princess rode me and brought us to rapture.

After four bouts of joining on the bed, on the dresser, and the wall, we decided to take advantage of the bath the maids had drawn for her. It was large enough for the two of us, and we took turns washing each other with the perfumed soap and cloth. Once we dried off, I carried her to the bed. We nestled beneath the covers, and her head rested against my chest.

"We made it." She sighed, and I wrapped my arm around her. I knew she meant to Crystoria, but we also had made it to this point together. I'd waited for her for over twenty years, and now we were snuggled in the large bed where we'd given our souls to one another.

"It's not over," I reminded her, and she nodded.

"Yeah. I wish we could stay longer, but there's too much at stake."

"We'll figure it out, together." I kissed the top of her head and listened for signs of the beast inside me. He'd been oddly quiet as I took Sapphira multiple times, content to enjoy the moans I had wrung from her body.

"Not regretting your decision? Being with me is a heavy burden." She peered up at my face, and I squeezed her for a second against me.

"The thought of dealing with your grouchy moods for the rest of our lives is a bit of a downer." I froze my face of any expression and waited. We knew I was the grouchy one between us, and my comment was only a jest.

"Yes, I'm the grouchy one." She smirked, and I couldn't hold my smile back any longer. "You have the most beautiful smile."

The awe in her voice could soften a cold heart, even mine.

"I don't deserve you." I admitted my most vulnerable thought as I lifted my other hand to brush her hair away from obstructing my view of her eyes.

"Then I shall just have to prove to you how false that statement is, no matter how long it takes." She grinned and settled against my chest once more.

"Good thing we are immortal," I huffed and closed my eyes, content to stay like this forever.

Chapter Thirty- Eight

Nyx

My sleepy eyes fluttered open and I focused on the unfamiliar stone ceiling above. Weak and weary, I turned my head and immediately messy brown hair came into my view.

"Tor?" I asked curiously, and the head lifted up and Tor yawned in my face.

"Ugh, bad breath." I coughed, watching as he smirked, then stretched.

"Yours doesn't smell like honey, either, Princess." He finished his long stretch and called to someone named Kryo.

"Where are we?"

"We're in Crystoria. Made it here in the late morning. The healers have fixed you up but said you would need to rest for the night." While he spoke, a man with long black hair wrapped in a braid and who wore white robes walked over.

"How are you feeling, young miss?" His voice was smooth, and his brown eyes crinkled around the corners. He had laugh lines, which I found soothing. A healer who laughed often was a healthy healer.

"OK, just tired and a little weak," I admitted and ignored Tor's stare. I didn't want to come off as weak but I knew I lost a lot of blood and there wasn't much I could do about it.

The healer nodded and asked if he could give my leg another look. I nodded and peered down as he did it. My pant leg had been cut off and there was a tan bandage wrapped around where I'd been shot.

"That is expected. You're going to need to rest for a few days. Your body is healing now that we've got you what you needed. I'll give you a salve you can rub into the muscles. It'll help keep infections away and soothe the pain." He grinned and set a small tin on the table next to the bed.

"She'll be all right, son." He patted Tor on the shoulder and walked away after rewrapping my leg. Tor grinned at the healer and I yawned. I felt like I'd slept for days and yet I craved more.

"I'm sorry, Nyx. I should have protected you more."

"You can't be serious," I said. What nerve he had to take credit for my battle mistake. His eyes narrowed and his mouth grew into a sharp line.

"Tor, none of this is your fault, and there isn't anything you could have done. We were all fighting, and this stuff happens."

"I could have—" I lifted my hand and pressed my fingers against his lips.

"No, you couldn't have and we aren't going to talk about the past. It's done. Let's move on, please," I pleaded and stared at him with tired eyes. Tor liked being the white knight to rescue the damsel. Sapphira didn't need him to be and right now neither did I.

"Seeing you unconscious like that scared me." His fingers gripped mine and moved them to his cheek. I gulped, unsure why he wanted my touch. Maybe my powers soothed him, and he wanted more.

"You seem OK," I said, doubting he was too beat up over me. He laughed and turned his face to press a kiss to my hand. It only lasted a second but the imprint on my skin warmed.

"I am now that you're OK."

He smirked and I pulled my hand back. He was acting strange and I didn't like the way my heart sped up from his attention. "Where are the others?" I changed the direction of our conversation, and he sat back in the chair he'd pulled close to the bed.

"They are at the palace with the queen, but I suspect they will be here soon. I saw one of the healers see you wake up and ran out the door to tell them." He looked gross, still covered in dried blood, dirt, and sweat. Had he stayed here since arriving in Crystoria? My eyes watered at the thought. Who was this man? Surely, not the joke-making, easygoing Prince Torin I knew. I averted my gaze once he looked at me again. My head was in a vulnerable place where I might say something I'd regret. Still, me and my big mouth couldn't help to speak my thoughts. I'd never been the best at keeping them in, anyways.

"You're a good male, Prince Torin." I peered to see if he'd crack a joke or bite back a laugh from my odd admission. Instead something I didn't expect happened. His head leaned down and he pressed a kiss to my lips. It was quick, and I stared with wide eyes as he lifted his head.

Thankfully, my friends entered the quarters, and I didn't have to say anything. Tor's knowing smile made me blush, and I squirmed.

"I'm so glad you're OK." Sapphira sobbed as she ran to my side, her hand searching for mine before interlacing our fingers.

I grinned. Something seemed different about her, and it was my job to know everything as her friend and handmaiden. I noticed a scab around her neck that looked like teeth marks. I shot a glance at Rune, who looked free and full of life, without a scowl. I waggled my eyebrows suggestively at the princess.

"I see you have been treated well since arriving in Crystoria."

Sapphira smiled wide but her cheeks turned red. Rune smirked and the others laughed. Even Tor chuckled. I'd wondered how he would react once Sapphira and his brother truly mated. Did he have eyes for me, or did he only kiss me because he couldn't have Sapphira?

I was no male's second choice.

Chapter Thirty - Nine

Sapphira

I excused the queen's maids to get ready for the feast on my own. I needed time to think, and their nervous energy distracted me. So much had changed in such a short time. I needed a moment to breath. However, my quiet time was short-lived when Dris pushed a wheelchair-bound Nyx into my room.

"We're here to help you get ready." They were already dressed in beautiful neutral-colored dresses. They sparkled and showed quite a bit of skin on both the ladies.

"Where are the maids?" Dris looked around and found no one flitting about the room to help me dress for the night. I shrugged and told them what I did.

"I just needed some time to think." I plopped on the bed and sighed. My friends came closer, and I appreciated their support.

"Emrys and I are sort of a thing," Dris squeaked, then covered her face with her hands. I laughed at her theatrics.

"I figured after I saw you tonguing his lip piercing." I giggled and patted her on the shoulder. Her hands fell

"We support you no matter what. Tor or no Tor." I squeezed her fingers one more time then withdrew my hand to rest in my lap. Dris sighed wistfully and did the same.

"We support you with Emrys, too." Nyx grinned at the owl Fae who blushed.

"Did you know that dogs sniff good-smelling things with their left nostril?" Dris babbled off a random fact, her go-to defense when she wasn't comfortable with a conversation. We laughed, and she flopped herself onto the bed dramatically.

"I'm crazy for being into him. Just after he fell down that trap door at Harold's Temple, I felt so many emotions that kissing him was the only thing I could think to do." The owl Fae spoke into the bed.

I liked seeing this side of both Dris and Nyx. They seemed so composed in their worlds. The librarian who chose books over males was now dating a mischievous spy. The particular princess who tried to control everything was now familiar with the uncontrollable world of men. Then you had me, winging everything as I go and mated to a temperamental warrior who housed a werewolf inside him.

"He's crazy about you, Dris." I spoke the only truth I knew about them. Emrys had always been enamored by Dris. He may be blood-sworn to me, but he would die to ensure she was happy.

"He is crazy." Dris rolled over and nodded.

"Speaking of crazy . . ." Nyx eyed me knowingly and I shook my head. Now the conversation had come around to me.

"Rune and I . . . mated . . . a few times...." I admitted and the girls laughed. They wouldn't be laughing if I told them about the pure bliss he wrung from me on the very bed.

"I'm glad you two finally came together, now there's no will they or won't they be together vibe between you." Dris patted me on the shoulder and I nodded. Even I tired from that whole agenda. Rune was mine, and I was his. Nothing would ever change that, not even death. We'd find each other in the afterlife and fall in love again and again.

"So was I right about the prickly on the outside, sweet on the inside?" Dris whispered her curiosity and Nyx and I chuckled.

"I love him."

Both girls gasped, then they sighed together. It was nice to say it out loud to someone other than my mate. It made it feel permanent and real.

Dris noticed the sun setting through the broad window and jumped off the bed. "We need to get you ready for the feast!"

"Nyx, you do her hair. I'll get the rest of her ready."

My two best friends raced to get me ready for the feast with my aunt. She'd promised it would be a fun night full of laughing, dancing, and stories about my father. I agreed to show only because I knew tomorrow would begin the next steps in our journey. We'd scour the great library for all information on the Heart Tree's whereabouts.

Chapter Forty

Sapphira

I officially loved my aunt and her wife.

When we first arrived, I was skeptical. I even turned green when I thought she had a thing with my general. Such a thing never happened, and now we were partners with a common goal. Play pranks on Rune. I'd never had so much fun in my life.

While I loved hanging out with my mother, she had always kept her grace and elegance. My aunt, however, burped like a man and had no issue getting dirty if the outcome was funny. Her mate, Queen Taraden, was the more composed one in their relationship. She was short, big in the hips, and had flaming-red hair. Her brown eyes rolled every time her wife told stories of how she relentlessly annoyed her brothers growing up.

"Nothing's changed. Still the annoying woman." Queen Dinesiri kissed her as punishment. An action that I could see Rune and I doing. In fact, I saw a lot of myself in her, and I yearned to know what I had in common with my father. From the stories Dinesiri told me, he was the warrior of the three siblings. He fought in battles, liked to drink alcohol after a great victory, and in his spare time enjoyed flying as a dragon.

"I loved it when he let me ride on his dragon form. So freeing to be in the air."

I nodded, knowing exactly what she meant.

When the two Queens danced on the floor, I couldn't take my eyes away. They were hopelessly in love after being married for fifteen years. Taraden was a demi-Fae. She'd been raised by her human mother but once she turned twenty, sought out her Fae father. He'd been a hawk Fae that lived in Crystoria. My aunt saw her one day while walking around the library and fell in love instantly. She courted the Fae, and when it was known Taraden shared interest in the queen, the mating bond snapped into place. Denisiri had only been queen for twenty years, and she'd done the best she could for her people. She'd been elected in the position after the previous king had fallen ill and died. Elections were something the Crystorian's preferred over the children of the throne inheriting the kingdom. My aunt would remain queen until she stepped down or died.

Dris loved talking with Queen Taraden about the library where she spent a lot of her time. They immediately bonded over their love of books until Emrys stole her away for a dance. I glanced around the room for Nyx and found her with Tor kneeling before her with his hand out. She nodded and he straightened back up. He stepped around the back of her wheelchair and pushed her onto the dance floor beside Emrys and Dris. There he began to spin her around and dance with her without a care in the world.

They were all so happy and tears crested my eyes.

"Mate." A growly voice vibrated against my back and I smiled. My body settled against his as he pulled me to his chest, his strong arms wrapped around my waist.

"I like seeing our friends so happy." Everything about this night warmed my soul. In this moment, life was great. I had an awesome aunt, my friends were in bliss, and I could be with my mate. It was like the dangers of the world didn't exist in this time.

"I'm glad Tor is enamored by someone else," Rune grumbled behind me, his lips pressed against the teeth marks on my neck.

"I think they make a good pair." I reached up to wrap my fingers around his neck. I wanted more of him. He chuckled against my neck and pressed another kiss to my skin. "You don't think he's just flirting with her because I chose you?" I had told Nyx I didn't think that to be true earlier, but doubts crept in. I feared her getting hurt.

"I think they are mates," Rune purred and nipped at my earlobe.

My fingers gripped him tighter. I watched them with hooded eyes to find what he saw. Being Rune's mate also meant being the mate of a werewolf. His very essence intensified what we shared. Nyx laughed as Tor danced with her in her wheelchair. I hoped Rune's suspicions were true. I wanted them both happy.

"He acted like a possessive asshole when Nyx was hurt, then protected her afterward. Sound familiar?" Rune teased, his fingers spread wide against my stomach, and my skin heated.

"Nope. Doesn't ring a bell." I moaned as he teased my body. Now that I knew what it was like to have him, it took every ounce of control I had not to drag him somewhere private. He rumbled against me, his hands pulling me into him and his very hard length.

"I thought we were bad when we first accepted the mating bond." My aunt and her wife danced by and I grinned. We didn't have to hide our love anymore, covering up longing glances or sneaking off to kiss in the dark. Rune and I could simply be together. Things were different this time, and I'd fight to keep it forever.

After a long night, everyone retired to their quarters. Rune tossed his bags in mine and declared we would be sharing a bed. I didn't fight him because let's face it, I wanted him with me. He soothed me and kept me safe while I slept. When we woke up, he lit my body ablaze in his possession of me. With every thrust of him inside me, my toes curled, and my insides quivered. Rune wasn't simply after sharing pleasure, he wanted to conquer me body and soul. I screamed as my release consumed every element of my being. He snarled as my sex clenched him with every shuddering wave of bliss I gladly endured. He swelled inside me and seconds later, he groaned against the side of my neck. I wrapped my arms around him and wished we could stay in bed like this for the rest of the day. I kissed the side of his head and enjoyed every little pulse of his release that sent shivers down to my toes then back up.

"I don't want to leave this bed," I whispered and squeezed him against me. Rune shook inside my arms, then lifted his head. I kissed his lips and squealed as he rolled us over with him still inside me. I laid against his chest and listened to his heartbeat.

"Claim you have bowel issues. I hear it's a perfectly good excuse when you wish to get out of duty." Rune's fingers ran up my spine tenderly. I glanced at his face with one eyebrow lifted and laughed when I saw his smirk. He was teasing me again.

"I think that will go over well. Sorry I can't save the world today. I've got bowel troubles." My mate was an idiot. I settled over him again while his chest shook from his laughter. We laid together for a few minutes before his gruff voice echoed within the stone room.

"What's with the box?"

I lifted my head to follow his gaze and saw my mystery box. An idea hit me as I remembered the contents resting in the velvety insides and hopped growling off of Rune.

"Stop your growling, I'm coming back." I grabbed the small ring and then dug through the little bag the maids had set on the dresser. When cleaning my armor and clothes, they'd come across Rune's ring and Tor's bracelet.

"It doesn't necessarily mean anything in the eyes of the kingdoms without an officiant, but I wanted to give you this." I ran back to the bed and snuggled under the covers with my naked mate. I set the sapphire ring on his bare chest and watched for his reaction. He eyed the jeweled ring I'd made for him twenty years ago.

"I found this in the box . . . a box I'd left on the roof of the palace back home for whenever I returned. I choose you, and this time I want everyone to know. No more hiding and dimming our bond. You are the best choice for me and for the future king—Crysia's finest general and protector of the people." I pulled the tiger's eye ring he gave me out and slipped it on my finger before his eyes.

"When we get the chance, I want to be yours in every way a woman can be."

I waited for him to speak, but he remained quiet.

"Rune—"

"Wife. You're going to be my wife." He snatched the ring and placed it on his finger. The jewel cooled my skin as he touched my face and pulled me in for a kiss. We had thirty minutes before we needed to meet up with our friends at the library, and Rune made every second praise-to-the-heavens worthy.

Chapter Forty - One

Tor

I liked to read but spending all day in the library was not my version of fun. We had to find the Heart Tree and heal it. Verin did something to it and then the human apocalypse happened while the Fae realm lost their magic. There were so many unknown variables.

The library itself was interesting, though. The only building taller than the library was the palace. The library housed five floors with grand staircases covered in long potted plants on the banisters. Stained glass windows, marble floors, and huge archways made of wood made it look like a cathedral instead of a library. There were pianos and various musical instruments placed in little garden rooms, where the plants absorbed the sounds to prevent echoing.

"Any luck?" Dris wandered to my table where I'd skimmed through two dozen books with nothing to show for it.

"Nope. I think I'm going to walk around and stretch my legs." I hadn't gotten much rest in months then had been mentally fucked over losing Sapphira. Now my thoughts bounced off the walls. I couldn't get the kiss I gave Nyx out of my head. Why did I do that? I tried to bring it up last night but she waved it off and told me to

Chapter Forty - Two
Sapphira

We'd been searching for hours and found nothing except a legend about the guardians of the tree. It was said that three sisters searched for the tree, but the tree found them unworthy. So it turned them into trees themselves, and they protected anyone else from finding it. A strange tale, and no one knew if they were rooted in truth or not.

Tor had came back from his walk with a wandering gaze like he'd seen a ghost. Rune sniffed the air as his brother walked by and silenced me with a glare when I started to ask Tor what had happened. Moments later, Nyx stomped by and sat on the table.

Before I could confront her, Rune growled at me. I narrowed my eyes at him, annoyed he kept trying to silence me. Obviously something had happened to them. Maybe they got in a fight, or he kissed her again. My mate leaned over and whispered so low no one else could hear.

"None of your business. Stay out of it."

He warned and I pursed my lips. Slowly, my focus darted to them and I looked for any sign of what occurred but saw nothing. They looked the same. There was no blood, only shocked and grumpy faces.

Dris had gone to another section of the library but came running back up the stairs.

"I think I found something!" She set an old scroll onto the table and we huddled around her.

"Two thousand and twenty-three years ago, a traveler came to Crystoria claiming to have been to a swamp between two crescent-shaped mountains. There he spoke to a red bulbous tree with vibrant blue leaves in the middle of the water." She scanned the scroll and I tried to read along with her, but the writing wasn't a language I recognized.

"What did the tree say?" Nyx asked, and Dris pointed to one section of the two-foot paper.

"He pleaded for the purpose of life, and the tree told him to live. Then he suddenly fell asleep in the water and woke up in the dry woods. His memory of how to get there was erased, but he goes on to describe the scenery at the tree down to the sulfuric scents. Sounds pleasant."

I sighed. Dris found amazing information, but it didn't tell us how to find this swampy place.

"Let's check all the maps we can find. It's got to be somewhat close to here." I sagged into my seat and imagined a red tree in a swamp like the traveler claimed to have seen. I was tired and needed some air. We could be in this library for days before we found anything definite. Hell, months even. That's if any evidence actually rested here. I breathed deeply and stood. Rune watched me curiously.

"I'm gonna go find my aunt. See if she knows anything else." I forced a smile and he nodded. The rest of my friends continued their search in the books while I walked away. The cool air greeted me as I stepped outside the magnificent wooden doors of the library. This place was beautiful, but I missed home. I missed my mother, her sweet smiles, and even the rambling she has been doing since I'd known her this time around. No one bothered me as I walked along the path to the palace. I'd hoped to talk with my aunt, but she and her wife were in a meeting with her army officials.

I'd try to claim a time spot with her later. My feet climbed the stairs and I mindlessly found myself at the door to my room. I wanted to go to bed, but I knew once my head touched the pillow, I wouldn't wake up for hours. I didn't have the luxury of time. The Dramens were clearly on the hunt for us. Did they know the location of the portals or their existence? I didn't have the answers. It was unnerving to say the least. Verin remained a large issue, and I feared the longer we took to restore magic, the greater his tenacity to stop me would grow. We hadn't seen any more soldiers since the one in the desert, but that didn't mean they weren't around.

What if he waited for us at the tree? What if going there meant walking into a trap? My head hurt. I placed my hands on the dresser and closed my eyes.

"You'll figure it out." I spoke to the empty room. When I opened my eyes, my focus landed on the box. I

215

lifted the lid, and sharp pain struck my middle finger. It lasted a second and a bead of blood bubbled and slipped off my fingerprint and onto the black paper.

I pinched my finger with my hand to stop the bleeding. I looked around the box for a clue as to what pricked me when I noticed a black line suddenly appear on the paper where my blood had landed.

"What the—" I mouthed and stared as the line grew darker. I forgot about the cut and grasped the paper. Besides that little mark, the rest of it was blank. I glanced at the blood and wondered if somehow my blood made the mark appear. Curiosity got the better of me. I lifted my finger to my canines to puncture the hole and blood coated my lips. It hurt, but I didn't care. I smeared my blood over the paper and waited.

Nothing happened.

Just as I was about to call myself stupid for hurting myself, little black dots broke through my blood. Words appeared, and it was in my handwriting. I gripped the paper harder and my eyes scanned each word delicately.

Dearest Me,

If you're reading this, then our plan worked, and you are now home once again. If you remember everything, then this letter is void. However, if you don't . . . if there were any side effects of Debaru's experiment, then you must hear the truth. Lachan is Verin, his core is obsidian, but his power is not what he tells everyone. He has no fire power. That gift belongs to his sister and our dad. His gift is poisons. I heard him talking to a young woman this morning. She is a portal jumper. She creates her own portals to travel among our realm. She kept telling him that she'd found it—the Heart Tree. He promised he would release a poison that would destroy everything. I pray we can stop him before it's too late. He has allied himself with the leader of Harold's Temple, and I fear they will strike once he has completed his plan. Sapphira, you have his power. You are the only one who can undo what he did. Go to Crystoria and follow the edge of the lake. Go into the mountains and you will come to a dark place where two crescent peaks come together. There will be dangers. The Heart Tree has protectors. The woman explained she couldn't get Verin too close. Be safe and welcome back to Crysia.

Love,

The old you.

Chapter Forty - Three

Sapphira

I raced back to the library to tell my friends what I found. They were stepping out of the doors and onto the stone steps leading to the road when I arrived.

"I found it!" I huffed loudly, then realized there were a lot of bystanders. Shit, we can't talk here. I took three deep breaths. "Let's go to the lake. I hear it's pretty." My group looked at me like I'd gone crazy. I gestured for them to follow me and pleaded with my gaze.

"Sounds good." Rune stepped to me and lifted his arm for me to take. The action was out of character, but I rested my hand on his arm and we walked leisurely toward the lake with our friends in tow.

"You're a terrible actress." He chuckled and I elbowed him in the side. The sooner we got to the lake where we could talk privately, the sooner we could be on our way. The lake behind the palace was only open to visitors on certain days, and luckily today wasn't one of them. The vast cerulean blue lake stretched on for a few miles. You could see the mountains behind it and hope thrived inside me.

"Sapphira, what did you find?" Dris asked.

"Before I took out my core, I wrote myself a letter, then put it in a box that I left on the top of the palace back home. At first when I opened the box, the letter was blank but then I accidentally dropped some blood on it and my blood brought the words out." I lifted the blood-smeared letter. Dris took it gingerly and read it aloud. As she did, Rune lifted my hand and inspected where I exaggerated the cut with my teeth. After inspection he deemed me OK and pressed his lips to the scab.

"Wow. This is big news."

"So we just have to go around this lake then look for the crescent peaks. I'm not sure about the danger part." Nyx stared at the paper then glanced to the mountains beyond the lake.

"We don't have much of a choice." I grimaced. Fighting off ancient protectors or defense mechanisms didn't sound fun. However, I'd do whatever I had to do for my people, all of them.

"When do we leave?" Emrys crossed his arms over his chest and grinned. My spider liked the adventure.

"Tomorrow morning. Let's rest. It's been a long day. If we go by the letter and the account of the traveler, we shouldn't have a far journey ahead." *Just a dangerous one.* I said that little bit in my head but I knew they were thinking it, too.

"I hate to be the skeptic, but can we trust the letter?" Rune asked.

I nodded. He looked at life from all angles, and it was a possibility that someone else could have put that letter in there since I didn't remember doing it. However, I just had that feeling I did it . . . a tug at something familiar in my mind that I couldn't yet reach.

"I trust it. I just have a familiar feeling I did it. Plus no one knew about the spot I hid the box or the contents." I eyed his hand where the Sapphire band glistened in the sun's rays. No one had said anything about the rings we adorned.

"Tomorrow it is."

We sat by the lake discussing our plans. Since we skipped dinner, we raided the royal kitchen where my aunt and Taraden sat eating ice cream with strawberries on top. We told her about the Heart Tree, and she warned about the stories of the guardians.

"I don't want anything to happen to you." She touched my cheek and continued eating. "Get some rest for the morning. I'll make sure your animals are ready and well-stocked for the journey." Her hands trembled, and I reached over to comfort her.

"I think I'm ready to go to sleep." Nyx yawned and rubbed her thighs.

"Same." Tor stood and stretched.

"I'm going to bed alone. Just so everybody knows," Nyx announced and everyone fidgeted in their seat. Well, everyone except Emrys who had a big smile on his dumb face.

"Same. Since we're announcing it to everyone." Tor smirked and glanced at Nyx, whose cheeks were bright red. She bid us all goodnight and stomped off dramatically.

"Am I missing something?" Dris watched our friend walk away.

"Night everyone." Tor chuckled and waved to us as he left.

"Oh, I remember those days." My aunt nudged her mate, and then laughed. Taraden smiled and pulled her queen in for a kiss.

I clearly was missing something like my owl friend.

"You telling me you can't smell it?" Emrys wrapped his arm around Dris, and her cheeks turned red like Nyx's.

This was the first time she'd allow any displays of affection in front of people. She looked so uncomfortable but she was trying.

"What smell?" She wrinkled her nose before sniffing their air.

"The mating bond smell." My aunt pulled away from her wife and took another bite of ice cream.

Mating bond smell? I pulled the shirt I wore up to my nose and sniffed it. Did we smell bad?

"I know what you're talking about, but Sapphira and Rune don't smell." Dris looked confused, and my face mirrored the same pinched expression.

"Not them. They've smelled that way ever since I knew them. You could tell Sapphira was never on the market, even as a human. Her bond with Rune was that intense. We're talking about Nyx and Prince Tor." Emrys had a shit-eating grin on his face, and it took a moment before his words registered.

My gaze immediately darted to Rune.

"Mate business is not our business. Stay out of it," he warned and now I understood why he was growling at me earlier.

Nyx and Tor were mates! How the hell did that happen?

"But I don't understand. Wouldn't they have felt it right away like we did?" I asked.

"No, my werewolf side intensified things for us. Torin is a demi-Fae. They experience the mating bond differently. Told you I thought they were." Rune smirked and eyed the ice cream Taraden had dug into. She noticed and handed him the carton with an extra spoon.

My mind reeled. Tor and Nyx were mates!

"Wait a minute . . . Oh no, not the library!" Dris covered her face. It hit me a few seconds later what she said and I burst into laughter.

"It's actually pretty fun to play around in there. Lots of secret places. The thrill of being caught at any moment," my aunt disclosed and her wife nudged her with her elbow.

"What? You never complain."

"Oh my God! The library! Books are sacred. People shouldn't have sex against them." Dris didn't care one bit that our friend was mates with Tor, only that they'd apparently done it against the books. I knew something was up when they came back from their walks. I hadn't been able to put my finger on it then, especially with Rune's attempt to keep me off the subject.

"Let her be. She'll come to you if she wants. We don't interfere with mate business," Rune warned me again, knowing my thoughts like they were his own.

"Fine," I said reluctantly. The conversation moved back to plans for our journey tomorrow. By the time Rune and I went to bed, my mind drifted back to thoughts of Nyx and Tor.

"Are you upset about them?" Rune pulled me to his chest, and I snuggled in.

"No. I think they will be good for each other." I found myself at peace with the news.

"I'm ready to leave. Ready to save the tree and release magic again."

"Soon. Now rest, wife." He kissed my head and closed his eyes. He was right. We needed rest. I couldn't stay up all night thinking about everything, or I'd be very tired tomorrow. I listened to his deep breaths and slowly allowed sleep to take me away.

Chapter Forty – Four

Nyx

We'd slowly been riding our animals past the lake for an hour, and I hoped we would reach the Heart Tree soon. I needed a break to escape Prince Torin. He'd been trying to talk to me all day and I cut him off every time. I didn't want to talk about us. I liked him and had wanted sexual release. I didn't think it would turn into something bigger.

Mates! He said I was his mate, and damn it to hell, I felt it, like some current running beneath my skin every time I got close to him. I wanted him.

"Why'd he have to kiss me?" I whispered to the trees. No matter how hard I wanted to deny it, I'd always been attracted to Torin. He was handsome with his blue eyes, fit body, and sexy run-your-fingers-through-it brown hair. He cared deeply and liked to live life on the cheery side. Why wasn't I jumping into his arms right now? I needed a moment . . . life had been moving so fast. I finally felt like I knew who I wanted to be, and where I fit in. Now I was someone's mate, and not just anyone, Prince Fucking Torin. Rune's brother, next in line for the throne in his kingdom, the ex-boyfriend of Sapphira. Hell, many people back home still thought they were engaged!

"You're overthinking things." The man of my thoughts snuck up on me, and I jumped on Persephone's saddle. He smiled and I wanted to kiss that smile off his face. I think he knew it, too, because his eyes turned a darker shade of blue.

"I don't wanna talk about this right now." I tried to brush him off again but he was relentless.

"Let's just take things slow and see how they go, OK?" He reached over to my reins and pulled, stopping both my horse and his unicorn. They neighed from the sudden stop but didn't put up a fight.

"Seriously, we are going to fall behind." I looked at our friends ahead and feared we'd separate from them.

"Right now, I don't give a fuck."

I was lifted off my horse and set onto his lap. I pushed against him, but he trapped my arms between our chests and slammed his lips against mine.

I melted and I hated how quickly I fell into him. All thoughts, all resistance I'd built overnight crumbled.

"Stop overthinking this. Let's just be. No pressure," he whispered against my lips. I wanted to kiss him for days, months, and never come up for air.

"Fine." I groaned as his tongue did that wicked swirly thing that I liked. I needed to push past my crazy and try to not obsess over what this meant for me, for us.

"One day at a time." He kissed me again, then assisted me in climbing back onto Persephone.

"I'm not good at that whole one-day-at-a-time thing. My brain is always on what's-next-and future mode," I warned, and he chuckled.

"Now come on, you really didn't have to be so demanding that we talk. Calm down, Nyx," he joked and the pleasant feelings inside me boiled into anger. I swear if this is what having a mate was like, I might smother him with a pillow. Mates shouldn't know your automatic triggers right away. Torin knew how to play me emotionally and physically.

"Feel better?" Sapphira sang softly as I rode up beside her, and I sighed.

"I can't tell if I want to kiss him or kill him." She nodded knowingly. I don't know how she dealt with these feelings. Multiple times, too! Their bond was more intense to boot. I think I'd never let Torin leave the bedroom if I felt as she probably did.

"He's def your mate, all right. I swear I'm always teetering that line with Rune."

"You're really OK with this?" I hated that I came off so self-conscious about her and Torin, but I was her handmaiden and friend. I cared how she felt.

"I really am, although I wish I would have gotten to celebrate with you when you told me. It's an exciting thing, and I think you compliment your own happiness well together."

She was right. Being with someone shouldn't take away your identity. They aren't the key to your happiness.

Happiness and identity come from within. Your partner only nourishes and compliments them. I could be with Tor and still be me.

"Thanks." I smiled at my friend, and the crazy in my head dimmed.

We walked in silence for another hour before the air grew warmer and the sky darkened, like a large cloud had settled in front of the sun, but there wasn't a cloud in the sky.

"Look! I think I see the crescent peaks." Dris pointed with glee at the two mountains that came into view, their jagged sides curved to a point.

"Keep an eye out for anything suspicious," Rune demanded and I grabbed my sword. We were so close, but we still faced possible dangers ahead. We needed to be ready. The closer we walked in the direction of those peaks, the short and uglier the trees grew. The ground slopped beneath Persephone's hoofs and an odor of rotten eggs crept into my nostrils.

"Perfect timing!" A harsh female voice echoed around the mountain sides.

A small red-and-black army stood between the two peaks, our only way to the Heart Tree.

Chapter Forty – Five

Sapphira

I pulled the reins on Cara, and she hissed at the armored soldiers ahead. I counted twenty of them, with a smaller woman standing in front. The red-and-black colors gave them away as Verin's forces.

"For a moment I thought we were going to have to wait all day to kill you. So gracious of you to arrive right on time." The female talked through her helmet, which was overkill, considering the rest of her armor was risqué for battle—thigh-high boots, a flimsy skirt, and a chainmail-cropped top over her small breasts. Tiny little thing.

"Who are you?" I demanded to know and reached for my axe. Rune already had his black blade in his hand, ready for a fight.

"I guess you wouldn't know me. Well, I think it's time we are introduced, cousin." The woman took off her helmet and straight black hair fell to the small of her back. She was pale, and her pointed face gave her an evil impression. *Wait... did she say cousin?*

"I am Lethirya, daughter of King Verin, ruler of the realms." She lifted her petite arms high, like divine light would shine down on her.

"Verin is no ruler of the realms," Emrys said from behind me, and I snarled his sentiment.

"Oh you are handsome," she purred, and Dris yelled a few profanities at Lethirya.

"You can't stop us," I stated to get her attention off my spider.

She laughed maniacally, and the birds in the trees flew away. Her eyes turned molten gold as she leveled me with a challenging stare.

"Let's find out," she laughed and whipped out a red sword from her hip and pointed it at us. Her soldiers roared and ran for us. They were Fae, and their speed and strength would surely match ours.

"Save your powers for the guardians, Sapphira." Rune launched into battle strategy to get us through these fools and to the Heart Tree.

"We will handle them. You two get to the tree," Nyx said and the others nodded. I didn't want to leave them alone to fight. We needed to do this together.

"Sapphira, let us help," Dris demanded and I relented. Rune and I would battle until we got an opening. We'd rush to the tree, then once it was done, we'd come back and finish off anyone who needed to be put down.

The soldiers were closer. Tor readied his bow, and then launched arrows at rapid speed. The men grunted as the arrow pierced the softs spots Tor saw in their armor, but they kept running.

"We'll see you soon," I told my friends. This was not goodbye; we would be back.

It was pointless to abandon our animals, knowing they would only return and fight with us. Cara growled at the men, and I unleashed her upon them. She lunged for the throat of the nearest soldier, and I thrust my sword to stab another. He dodged my blade with ease but ran straight into Rune's blade.

I was so focused on the two men coming for me that I missed the woman flying at me from the trees above. Her boot hit me in the chest like a weighted hammer. I flew off Cara and violently coughed.

"The Chosen One. Ha! You can't even stay on your ride." She slung her red blade at me, and I blocked her with my own sword.

"I hear a bit of jealousy in your voice," I baited her, much like how Rune used to do to me while we trained. I'd get into a fit of rage that I'd make mistakes. I hoped she would fall for it, too.

"Jealous of you. Never. I am the princess the world will remember. I was born to a realm of monsters and darkness. I am their master. You are a pitiful mistake that whore you call a mother sired with the wrong man."

She spit at me and kicked her heel toward me. I jumped and whirled my sword over my head. She came at me with precise swings and calculated hits. She had trained and trained hard for this. I could admit she was better than me with a weapon. Had I not become a human and lost my memory I could have bested her in minutes.

But I wasn't that warrior Sapphira from the past. I was a new beast, and I had fangs.

Flames coated my blade as hers clashed against it. Embers flew in all directions and I took advantage of the distraction and threw my head into hers. My brain shook but I had my opening, however short. Rune appeared at my side and helped me to my feet.

"Time to go."

Cara and Silvio saw us moving toward the peaks and ran to our aide. We climbed on and pushed them into their fastest speed. I glanced back at our friends and saw weapons clashing against each other. They'd be OK. I knew it in my gut.

Lethirya had hopped onto a massive red lizard with spikes around its head and chased after us.

The ground slushed beneath our beast's feet the farther into the swamp we raced. The tree had to be here somewhere. Up ahead, three massive trees stood close to a slit in the cliff.

"The Heart Tree has to be on the other side of that cliff." I pointed toward it. But the closer we got, the appearance of the trees near the rock changed. The trunk wobbled and ballooned like something inside of it moved. Roots wiggled against the ground and arm-shaped bark began to slither down the massive trunk. Slowly, a snapping sound shot through the swamp as three giant woman-shaped masses burst from the trees as if they were the soul within the trunks. They took a step in our direction.

"The guardians." I breathed as the tree woman on the right grew a large spear in hand and threw it right at us.

Chapter Forty – Six

Sapphira

"Dodge!" I screamed, and Cara and Silvio moved out of the spear's path, but they'd almost been too slow. The three guardians took another step toward us, and I angled my head around them to see the opening. It was narrow, big enough for us and our animals but not these tree women.

"Use your fire, Sapphira!" Rune bellowed as another giant splinter shot past us and embedded deep into the mud.

"You won't get past them. Turn back now and face my sword!" Lethirya screeched behind me. She'd stopped chasing us a while back. Probably too afraid to face the guardians or hoped we'd die trying to get through them.

"You are not a worthy challenge, unlike these ladies," I hollered back, enjoying her frustrated scream as I deemed her unworthy for a fight. The bitch had issues.

We were about one hundred feet away and the closest guardian swung her large tree-like hand. I willed my hand to burn and to release the fires in me. Flames jumped from my fingers to hers and the guardian screamed so loudly, I had to cover my ears. The woman flailed and dug her hands deep into the mud to coat the blaze that spread across her wood body. The others lunged for us, and Cara gripped one of the wood bodies with her claws and climbed up its arm.

I gripped Cara with all my strength as she jumped from one body part to another to get over the guardian. Silvio stood up on two feet with Rune standing on the saddle. The bear had grown silver swirls from its chest that wrapped around its furry body. The bear roared at the third guardian and I could see the sound move across the air and shatter the wood with every wave.

A wooden hand smashed onto the shoulder in front of us, and Cara leaped over it. I might not have chosen this route, but Cara was quick and lithe as she avoided being hit by the flailing guardian.

Arrows shot past my head in a woosh. I glanced back. Lethirya had dared to come closer with a large black bow. I hated that side of the family so much. Estranged creepy cousin and her evil father who raised me instead of her. I could see why she hated me, however, Verin obviously made her into his own image as the vicious creature she stood today. An arrow sliced into my shoulder, and I lost my grip of Cara. My body slipped from hers and bounced off the hard wood body, then slid down a leg. I landed in the soggy and smelly mud. It coated the whole front of me and I scrambled to my feet as a large guardian root foot slammed two feet away from me.

"Shit!" I cursed and lunged as the guardian tried her hardest to flatten me into the earth. I threw flames at the ancient wood and her sister covered her in mud, instantly putting it out. Double crap.

"Sapphira!" Rune ran to me on foot and tackled me into the mud as Silvio roared again. Wood splattered against Rune's back, and he grunted into my neck with every blow.

"Come on." He grunted through his pain and helped me climb to my feet. We ran and saw Cara and Silvio do the same toward the narrow cliff entrance. A guardian reached for us and Rune slashed her fingers with his sword. She screamed, and I cried from the pain in my head. I didn't know how much longer we could take this.

"Earth. Use it." Rune grit his teeth as he ran fast, almost dragging me with him.

I extended my hand and took a deep breath. Mud tentacles shot out and wrapped around the guardians' limbs.

"It won't hold them for long."

I didn't have endless amounts of each power inside me. I could use them but there was a limit. The longer I touched the person, the more of their essence I absorbed. Rune and I touched a lot so I had more of his than some others. I'd barely begun to reach my well of powers, and I forgot how to use most of them. Like my mother's diamond skin.

I willed my skin to turn hard, and impenetrable just as a large wooden hand came for us.

"Fuck," Rune cursed as the hand hit us so hard our faces slammed into the stone wall of the cliff. Blood filled my mouth and I spit into the mud. I bit my cheek and my head ached so badly I thought my vision would turn blurry. So much for diamond skin. Silvio and Cara ran into the narrows that stood fifteen feet away from us. We darted for the divide but a hand gripped Rune as we took one step into the safe haven.

"No!" I screamed, and flames erupted from my body. I wasn't going to lose him, not now, not ever. The cliffs shook and rock started tumbling from the top on the guardians' heads. Rune grunted as the hand around him squeezed harder and I threw a line of fire like a rope around the wood wrist. The tree woman shrieked from the burn and dropped Rune. I ran to him and lifted his arm over my shoulder. He could lean on me as he needed. We were so close.

The guardians were busy fighting off my mud tentacles and once we finally made it into the slice of the cliff, I shot up a stone wall so they couldn't try to grab us. Rune and I collapsed onto the muddy grass, and our animals nudged their faces in ours.

"We're OK." I comforted them as Cara purred against my head. Silvio breathed in Rune's face, and he nudged him away.

"I'm fine you, mother hen." He shook his head, and Silvio dropped down beside us, splashing mud onto our legs.

"Thanks, bud." Rune leaned his head against the stone wall, and I looked him over for injuries. We needed to get out of this mud or any cuts like the one on my shoulder could get infected.

"We need to keep moving." I gripped Cara's drooping reins. She lifted her head and helped pull me up. My muscles burned and sharp pains shot from various parts of my body. Rune rose to his feet and gripped my hand.

"Together."

I nodded. Whatever we found at the end of this narrowed canyon, we'd face it as one.

Chapter Forty - Seven

Sapphira

The ground hardened, then grew wet as we walked through the divide. There was nothing between these cliffs except us and stone. No wind and no sounds.

"I hope the Heart Tree is ahead." What if everything we went through was for nothing?

"It is." Rune squeezed my hand and I breathed deeply.

I needed to keep a level head. Our friends, families, and kingdoms depended on me.

"Something feels off." Rune let go of me and knelt to the ground.

I did the same, but I only felt rock. He stared ahead, one hundred percent of his senses on something unseen.

"Rune?"

"We're close," he whispered, and took off into a sprint. I chased after him and so did our animals. About thirty yards from me, he stopped, his feet in the ankle-deep water.

"What is it?"

The divide opened into a large circular space with the sun beaming through a red-and-white crystal ceiling. The dry ground spiraled around the circle and ended with a tree on an island in the middle.

The Heart Tree.

I could barely breathe, my heart beat wildly in my chest. We did it. I stared at the tree of legends with my mouth agape and wide eyes. It was about twenty feet tall with bright blue leaves sparkling in the light. Its trunk was swollen with thin membranous tissue surrounding it, like a pregnant belly, if a tree could be such a thing. A gray light shined from where the roots dipped into the water.

I took a step closer and the whole area turned deep red. Rune unsheathed his sword and I grabbed the only axe I had left. Nothing else happened and we took another step closer.

"Sapphirrraaaaa." A whisper flew on the random breeze that tickled my mud-caked curls. The voice sounded like the eerie wind of Celestine's cave that forever called to me.

"Did you hear that?" I turned to Rune and he nodded, his stoic expression taking note of our surroundings.

"Sapphiirrraaaa."

"I am here, Sapphira of Crysia."

Then I heard a familiar meowish hoot.

"No fucking way that should be here." Rune growled and I stared at the tree to where one of Celestine's owl cats sat, its tail wagging against the branch.

"Celestine?" I called to the tree, and I looked for the seer. If she was here, I swear I might punch the woman on principle.

Sure enough, the hooded black-haired owl Fae appeared out of thin air. Pissed, I marched right up to the woman and threw a mean right hook right at her pale face. My hand moved through her as if she was made of air, and momentum took me to the ground.

"Explain!" Rune bellowed, as he rushed to my side and helped me up. Our animals stayed near the edge of the spiral and laid down with their attention on us.

"It's nice to see you too, General." Celestine became solid again, and a root lifted from the ground at the perfect height for her to sit on.

"When I was a young woman, I traveled to the Heart Tree in search of truth. I flew in as my owl form and the guardians didn't pay me much mind. I'd always been connected to the land and the spirit world. I had visions of the future, but they were random images in my dreams."

A foreshadowing settled in my gut. Wherever this tale would go, I knew it would demolish everything I thought I knew.

"Back then, the Heart Tree was full of life and sparkled with red lights. Its seeds would fall into the water and a new Fae would be born in the world with the gifts chosen for the greater good. I'd been deemed worthy, and the Heart Tree spoke to me." One of her owl cats jumped to the root, and she rubbed its purring head.

"It could see all the futures, until the end of time. It needed my help, and in return, I gained the gift of truth. I could see all, and I became the voice for the tree. Then Verin came. The Prince of Poisons pretending to be someone else to win Queen Olyndria's heart. The tree knew he would be its ending and so we came up with a plan." The seer smiled grimly at me, and my knees wobbled.

"You'd been conceived by a love as pure as the Heart Tree itself. Desmire and Olyndria were supposed to rule together and unite all the kingdoms in peace with the humans. But the devious king tricked your mother, and she married him instead. But he couldn't stop love. The tree chose you as its champion to fight Verin and to be the leader of all people. I gave you the hints. I told you you were to find Debaru's books so that you would choose to place your sapphire's core in the safety of the onyx. The king traveled with his daughter, the portal jumper, to this sacred place and poured a toxic blend of his most powerful poison with acid into the waters that feed the tree. It sparked against magic and cut off all connections to the life forces of our world." She sighed, her hand reaching to rub her neck, as if she could feel pain constricting her soft skin.

"He didn't know that the tree also feeds into the human realm. The sparks jolted into the human realm and the poison polluted the air. Its darkness shot across the sky and everything electrical stopped, including the hearts of humankind. After the queen tampered with the memories of all who knew you, Verin thought he had won. He came to me to gloat and sliced my throat so I couldn't help the queen anymore."

I thought I would collapse but Rune held me. She'd been dead for twenty years.

"My body absorbed into the ground and the Heart Tree brought my spirit here. It still needed me, to wait for you, and prepare you for your destiny."

"What is her destiny?" Rune asked the question I wanted to know but couldn't speak.

"To kill the Heart Tree."

The seer touched the bark of the tree and the swollen trunk flickered. I noticed a blackness crept into the tiny veins that filled the tree with life.

Chapter Forty – Nine

Tor

Verin's guards were stronger than the Dramens we'd fought, but the differences ended there. They were just as angry, as well as blinded by their inclination for blood and power. We'd taken down ten but the other ten had waited for the others to waste our energy before they attacked. We were tired, and Dris suffered a blow to the back that sent Emrys on a killing rage. Nyx managed to sidestep every soldier and slice a blade as she moved.

I pulled the string on my bow back and released it into the thigh of a guard running toward her from behind. They were getting smarter about protecting their weak spots from me. I glanced in the direction Rune and Sapphira had ridden. It felt like they'd been gone for hours, but I knew time hadn't flown that fast. Her cousin chased after them but as I looked for our princess, I saw her riding a red monster toward us.

Shit.

The female was small but lethal. I wouldn't abandon Sapphira or my brother and retreat. We needed to handle this, give them time. A fist landed on my distracted face, and I fell back for a second, then dodged as the soldier came at me with a knife in his left hand. I blocked it with my forearm shield and pushed him back a foot. I quickly gripped an arrow and kicked his feet from beneath him and drove the pointed tip into his throat as he fell to the ground.

"Tor, watch out!" Nyx screamed and I rolled away just in time as a red blade came down where I'd just kneeled.

"Prince Torin," Lethirya purred and lunged with her sword toward me. Shit. I grabbed a loose helmet and lifted it to block her blade. The force behind her swing reverberated down my arms.

"Your brother and the princess are dead. Pity the guardians had the pleasure of killing them instead of me." She sneered and flipped high above me and I rolled over, bringing a dead soldier with me for protection as her blade pierced her dead. No remorse for these expendable warriors. She'd probably kill them all if they stood in her way. However, I could feel the lie spewing from her lips this time.

"You lie." I jumped to my feet as she struggled to put her weapon from the dead soldier's armor.

"They died in each other's arms, if that makes you feel better." She screeched while I tackled her as she pulled her blade free. Punching a woman wasn't cool, but this bitch was going to do real damage if I didn't take her out. She growled like a feral animal and thrashed beneath me. I pinned her to the ground and reared my fist back and the ground shook violently. Everyone stopped fighting as the air sparkled and then we were all blown back by a blast.

My body tingled and I scrambled to look for Nyx and our friends who lay on the ground.

"NO! This isn't over." Lethirya's shrill scream wrecked my ears.

She crawled to her feet and her soldiers followed her. They stood twenty feet away as she looked down at her trembling hands.

"I feel strange." Dris clutched her stomach. Nyx and she seemed to be OK besides a line of blood dripping down the left side of her face.

A ripping noise echoed around us, and Lethirya insanely laughed as her hands sparked and a round swirling portal grew around her body.

"You may have won this round, but now the odds are even." She grinned and fear shuddered down my spine. Her remaining soldier disappeared through the portal, which widened as her red monster walked through.

"See you next time, Prince." She grinned at me and then winked at Emrys before she snapped the portal closed. They were gone, having left through a magical portal.

Magic.

"Guys!" Emrys called to us, but I couldn't see the goat Fae from where I sat on the ground.

"Where are you?" I slowly climbed to my feet and searched for the male.

"Over here," he called from my right but he wasn't there. Suddenly, his body appeared and I cursed.

"I have my powers back. They did it!" Emrys hollered in rejoice and hugged Dris.

"Can you shift?" he asked her, and she shook her head.

"I can feel it, though. The connection to my owl side is stronger. It probably just takes some time." She grinned before her lips connected with his. Their joy was contagious. I walked to Nyx and helped her off the ground to inspect her wounds. Nothing too serious, the head tended to bleed dramatically even with a small cut like hers.

"Are you OK?" She gripped my probing hand and pulled it to her cheek. She cradled my hand against her warm skin and my heart softened for her. She'd been through so much and had a big wall around her heart. But this tender gesture gave me hope.

"Yeah. I'm good." I kissed her sweet lips. I'd show her that we could be good together. That we'd fight, and be stubborn, but we could also turn that fire into pleasure.

"I think I see them!" Dris exclaimed, and Nyx pulled away from our kiss to scan the grounds for Sapphira and Rune.

"I see them, too."

Rune and Sapphira were covered in bruises, mud, and bits of blood as they neared us.

"Sapphira!" Nyx called out to her princess, her hand waving in the air excitedly. Five minutes later, they stopped a few feet from the battle scene where we stood and slowly descended their mounts. Nyx and Dris ran to Sapphira and swallowed her body into a group hug. Emrys disappeared, and I huffed, knowing he was going to screw with Rune in some way.

"Welcome back, best friend," Emrys said next to Rune, but my brother didn't jump. He grabbed the air and pulled it downward.

"OK! OK! I won't pat you on the back again!" Emrys howled and then his head became visible in Rune's hold. He could probably hear Emrys's steps and breath.

"You guys did it." I walked up to Sapphira and joined in on the group hug that still clung tight, then moved to my brother and stuck out a hand.

"Magic has been released." In a move that surprised everyone, he grabbed my hand and pulled me in for a brotherly hug. What the hell happened at the Heart Tree? He released me seconds later and smirked at Sapphira.

"Let's get back to Crystoria, then head home." Sapphira pulled back from her friends and smiled at them. Something was off. Maybe it was the way Sapphira's smile didn't reach her cheek, or the sagging posture of her shoulders. Rune drew closer to her and placed his hand on the small of her back for comfort.

253

"I am so ready for a long bath." Nyx nudged me with her shoulder. The image of Nyx and I in the bath together pushed whatever occurred between Sapphira and Rune into the back of my mind.

We rode the long hours back to Crystoria without much talking, and I couldn't shake the eerie sensation in my gut. When we finally arrived in Crystoria, the city was in disarray. Golden-armored soldiers were directing the people to the palace and the library for their safety.

Queen Denisiri stood at the bottom stairs to her palace in pants and a feathery, gold, armor top.

"Aunt Denisiri! What's going on?" Sapphira hopped off Cara and ran to her aunt.

"Oh my sweet dear. I'm glad you are safe, but I fear we don't have much time. The Dramens have breached the portal. They will be here by dawn. It's time to prepare for war." The queen hugged Sapphira briefly before hurrying after her generals to talk battle.

"Friends, we need to talk." Sapphira glanced at Rune and then looked at us.

Chapter Fifty

Sapphira

Rune and I decided not to tell our friends about the baby. We needed time to truly digest the news ourselves along with the weighted destiny that came with it. We grabbed my aunt and her general and told them about the Dramen king and queen's real identity. Everyone gasped and realized we weren't just up against war hungry humans, but a mixture of Fae, demi-Fae, and humans. Magic had been released and that meant both sides would use it to their advantage.

Some Fae's powers immediately returned after we'd burned the Heart Tree. For others, it returned slowly. Dris hadn't been able to shift into an owl yet, but she claimed her bones ached and her skin tingled. I hoped she returned to her natural self soon. The scouts had given us till the early morning hours before the Dramens marched on Crystoria's borders. All the farmers closest to the portal had been evacuated along with the people who couldn't fight. The palace and the library were safe havens for everyone.

As much as I tried to get some rest, my mind raced. I was going to be a mother, and my baby would have the gifts of the Heart Tree. Dramens were here for war, and I hoped I could protect not only myself and my loved ones, but the people of this kingdom.

Rune maybe got an hour's rest before he gave up and went to work alongside the Queen. Once I rose, I met my friend's uneasy stares in the kitchen and we ate in silence. Then our group split as we changed into new armor that hadn't already seen a fight, and grabbed new weapons.

"You look good in gold." Rune breathed against my neck; his hands spread across my stomach. The male could barely stop touching me since he'd heard the baby's heartbeat. I dressed in the golden armor plates with white drapery across my hip. I attached a sword into my hip scabbard, two knives into my knee-high boots, and two hatchets on my thigh holsters. I twisted in my mate's arms and curled into his arms.

"Be safe, my moon." Rune approached me and rested his head on top of mine. I breathed in his scent. I was grateful my mate wasn't going to lock me up now that I carried his child. When I asked him how he felt about me fighting, he had kissed me deeply and said, "There is no one else I trust more to keep our babe safe than you, even on the battlefield."

"Do you feel your powers yet?" I asked, as we walked down the halls of the palace. Soldiers were running around, getting ready for the upcoming battle. I glanced at my mate as we neared the main doors that led to the front courtyard.

"It's a surprise." He smirked and I rolled my eyes. Leave it to Rune to make a dramatic entrance. Our friends were dressed similar to us in gold. They'd taken the news of Harold and his Dramen army fairly well. However, we had no clue what we were about to face. A horn blew in the distance, and we ran for our beasts. My aunt had armor suited over them as well, protecting their hides from spears or arrows. We rode to the edge of the city and through the opening of soldiers to where the queens sat on top of their mounts. Crystoria had a massive army of seven thousand Fae.

"Was that you?" I asked, as I reined Cara to a stop in the line beside my aunt. She looked like a goddess with her armor and a golden crown on her helmet. Her tattoos glistened like fire beneath her skin. She had the gift of flames like my father, so maybe it truly did.

"It came from the trees ahead." Queen Taraden grabbed her white bow and readied an arrow. She was dressed similarly to my aunt, except she refused a helmet, claiming it blocked her vision.

"They're here." My aunt sat taller on her white-and-gold unicorn mare. The air quieted and no one moved as we waited to see the army who had come to this peaceful land looking for war.

"To the left!" Dris pointed and a herd of deer leaped from the forest line and ran fast. Slowly, one by one, men and women dressed in fur and feathers stepped into view. Their army spread wide and deep, their iron weapons glistening in the sun. Gun shots echoed across the roads and field as the Dramens celebrated making it this far. I hoped they wasted all their bullets.

"We're going to push them in and fire arrows as they near. Our armor should hold against their weapons. However, be leery of magic," my aunt declared and I nodded. Their strategic plan had been flawless. Even Rune was impressed with how they planned to deal with this attack. But first, she would ride into the middle with her general and Rune to meet with Harold and whoever he brought with him. She'd try to make peace, but if none could be found, then we'd fight.

"I love you, Tara." The queen looked to her wife and they clasped hands.

"We'll have celebratory ice cream once this over." Taraden smiled and squeezed Densiri's hand twice before letting her mate go.

"Stay here. Wait until we've returned." She commanded and her soldiers banged their weapons against their mighty shields. I noticed the emblems on them and examined the delicate carving of a tree with its crystal leaves in the wind with an owl sitting on a branch.

Rune touched my leg briefly before nudging Silvio forward to walk with the queen. Pride grew inside my chest instead of fear as I watched my mate walk toward the massive army. My warrior, a legend who would defend this kingdom like it was his own. He was fierce and unmatched among the land. I pitied any of the Dramens who veered into his path.

"They'll be OK." Nyx sat beside me on Persephone, and I tried to smile even in the electric atmosphere.

"I know they will."

Five figures rode into the front of the army on horses. The king looked like the dangerous man I'd seen at the iron city. His blond hair was braided back and the sides of his head were shaved. He had tattoos along his neck and a shiny iron spiked crown sat on his head. His queen rode on a brown horse, her leather and fur hiding the feral woman I knew she was. Her black-spiked crown looked like a weapon itself.

The air became still and silent, as we waited to see what came from this meeting.

I heard shouting and then a gun shot. Suddenly, flames burst between them and spread like wildfire to the edge of the forest line.

"What happened?" Taraden called to her queen as they rode full speed back to where we waited. A dent stood out in the queen's golden armor and I actually growled. They'd shot her. Assholes.

"Harold has come to take over the Fae realms. Verin convinced him that the Fae who caused the apocalypse were all dead. That the portals were broken. When you arrived at the Iron City to save Prince Torin he knew he was misled."

"We go to war."

A chill ran down my spine.

Chapter Fifty - One

Sapphira

There are times in life when you look back at everything you've done and wondered how it could all lead to now. I had one of those moments as my aunt marched her unicorn down the lines of her army and inspired the warriors to fight for their land, for their families, and against tyranny. As the Dramen army ran for us, I didn't cower. I couldn't escape my fate, but I could fight like hell to be the woman I wanted to be. I could be brave like my mother, inspiring like my aunt, strong like my father, and determined like my mate.

My aunt's fire had done its job, and the bloodthirsty fools bottlenecked into the middle. The archers fired their arrows and the first round of Dramens fell to the ground. The next round of arrows released and then another. No matter how many we shot into the sky, more Dramens came.

They fired their powerful guns, and the bullets landed about twenty feet away. Thankfully we had some power of our own. Large boulders on catapults were launched, and the stones flew through the air and landed on Dramens as they crashed to the ground. The dirt kicked up and twisted in the air.

"Shit, that's the power of wind." Taraden cursed and a winding tornado formed and circulated toward us.

Someone on the other side was playing with their liberated magic. The air whipped around us, but the soldiers remained in formation. However, when the ground began to shake, the army murmured their worries. A fissure in the earth cracked and spread toward the Dramen leaders sitting on their horses. Dramens screamed as they fell to their deaths, and the tornado died as their army became distracted.

I glanced at my mate and watched as he smirked. I swear that smirk made me want to tackle him to the ground right there in front of everyone.

"Sapphira, really? I think you can resist your urges for now." Nyx laughed from my side and I blushed.

Roots broke from the ground and pulled the king and queen away from the chasm. While we watched Rune's dramatic crack in the earth seal up after missing his target, the soldiers on our outskirts yelled. Soldiers had sneaked beyond the queen's firewall and were closing in. Some of them transformed into animals—a bear and a mountain lion to our right and a large lizard to our left.

"Soldiers! To war!" The queen lifted her sword to point at the darkening sky then thrust it forward. Our warriors broke into a run. The outer rim clashed with the Dramens. Once our soldiers were about to meet the opposing army, my aunt pushed her wall of fire into the

Dramens. Some burned and some were able to block the blaze from scorching them. A strong wind swept into her flames and twirled them around and around until it was contained in a tight fireball. The wind Fae threw the ball toward us, and Rune lifted a large sheet of rock into the air to deflect the flames.

"Time to fight." Rune looked at me once before nudging Silvio into a run. The queens rode into battle with their soldiers, and it was time for us to follow.

"Be safe, my friends." I spoke loud enough for my friends to hear over the roars of battle.

"Run, Cara!" My catagaro pushed off, and I held tightly to the reins. It seemed whatever magic we threw at the Dramens, they had someone in their ranks to offset it. Rune battled with an unseen enemy in the masses that would grow a tree or a thick vine as he tossed a boulder. Finally, he'd roar and the tree would sink into the ground before the battle continued.

As the soldiers clashed, gun shots rang, and swords clanged against iron weapons. I pressed my hand against my stomach and was thankful for the diamond armor I'd slipped on under the golden chest plate.

"To a better world for you," I whispered to the babe. Cara leaped into the crowd and I slashed my sword as she pounced and chomped on the Dramens who neared us. A gun shot hit my helmet. I roared with rage and grew fire within my hands. One by one I threw the fireballs at the nearest Dramens and their screams were music to my ears.

"Conserve your power!" I heard Rune yell at me from a few yards away where he sat on Silvio and shot arrows at rapid fire. He was right, of course, but I threw a few more for spite. We were beating back the Dramens and magic was thrown from both sides. Shifters fought shifters, the elements battled, and humans fired bullets. Blood splattered everywhere and people's sliced limbs were scattered next to dead bodies.

An explosion blasted, sending me and Cara into the air. We landed hard against a group of our soldiers and I cried out for my beast. She laid on the ground a few feet away from me and didn't move.

"You killed my Cara!" I blared, and rushed into the battle with a ringing in my ears. I slicked every Dramen that raised a weapon to me, and I used every bit of fire and earth power I could. Men were sunk into the ground, where they'd suffocate or burn to death. I gripped at the poison gifts from Verin inside me and touched the face of a Dramen wearing a bear skull on his head. His veins turned green from my caress and he foamed at the mouth. I threw my hatchet into the skull of a Dramen whose gun pointed toward me. Tor pulled it out before his outstretched arm hurled it into a Dramen who'd crept behind me.

"Thanks!" I smiled at him and plucked the hatchet from the dead soldier. We managed to beat them back into the forest, and a snowy owl flew along the line of the trees. Dris had shifted into an owl and scoped the enemy. Arrows were fired at her and she dodged them with expert maneuvers to the right and left. We were winning. I pressed my hand against my baby belly again, thankful we'd managed to win this war so quickly. Cheers of celebration filled the air only to die into silence seconds later.

I stared at the forest where our soldiers had chased the remaining sum and gasped. Our warriors were blasted apart as large metal tanks rolled onto the scene.

Chapter Fifty – Two

Sapphira

Cars didn't work, and planes had dropped out of the sky in the human realm. Everything electric died during the apocalypse. Yet, the Dramens had found a way to make ten tanks roll across the ground and fire massive bullets at us. Large elephants trumpeted as they pounded the ground toward us with Dramens on top, firing weapons as fast as they could.

"Fall back!" my aunt roared to her subjects to put some distance between us and the war machines coming for us. Steam billowed out of a stack in the side of the steam-powered tanks.

Strong winds whipped into us, and Dris swirled in the gusts overhead. Dirt flew into our faces, and I could barely see a few feet in front of me. Shit. Shit. Shit.

BOOM!

A shot from the tank sounded like a damn cannon. I heard an explosion to my right and golden soldiers were blown into the air. I wanted to call for my friends, to make sure they were OK, but I didn't want to distract them. A root grabbed my foot, and I sliced at it with my sword. More grew from the ground and tangled over my body. I lit my hands on fire as a metal tank rolled into my view. If I didn't move, it would mow me over. The roots burned but ten grew in its place. Think fast, Sapphira.

I closed my eyes and sucked in a breath when the tank was three feet away. I willed myself to sink into the ground. The clashing of blades and guttural screams became silent. I only heard the rumble of the machine and feet above the ground. Once the tank had moved on, I shot up and burned the roots who tangled me to ash. I knew I had a chance to do some damage on that tank, so I raced to it and jumped on the metal hood. I slammed my hand on the metal in anger and surprisingly it dented like I'd dropped a boulder on it. My focus shifted to my skin, shimmering I'd been dusted with a jewel that had hardened—my mother's diamond power.

When in battle, she was purely indestructible. She could turn her skin into a diamond and was extra strong, nothing could hurt her. I'd absorbed some of that from my mother and I mentally thanked her for the extra protection for the babe in battle. My body was a safe haven. I punched the metal and it clanged against my hit. After two punches I was in. I set the innards of the tank ablaze and Dramens yelled. I melted the seal and trapped them inside.

"You bitch," someone screamed and a sword swung at my face. A purpled-haired goddess jumped in front of me and stopped the blade with her own.

"You smell." Nyx flung a silly insult at the female Dramen and sliced her with her Fae speed.

"Thank you, Nyx. You OK?"

She nodded, her breaths heavy from the fight.

"Behind you!" she yelled, and I twisted around with my hatchet in hand. It took three seconds to reach its target and the dead Dramen fell to the ground. I hopped over the melted tank and rolled to the ground to retrieve my sword.

As I stood, I scanned the battleground. Dramens kept flooding the scene. We were outnumbered, and even with powers, there was a chance we might not win.

"What do we do? They just keep coming." Nyx stood by my side, and I didn't have an answer. I wasn't in charge and I was glad of it. Queen Denisiri had to make life-or-death choices for her whole kingdom. I winced knowing that sooner or later, I'd have to do the same.

The queen fought in the middle of three Dramens. She'd harnessed her flames into a whip and slashed it around like she'd practiced the moves for centuries. When her eyes locked with mine, she whipped the flames around the neck of a Dramen and the fire cauterized the head off.

"We need more soldiers!" she yelled.

We were running out of options. The ground shook to our right and Rune had collapsed five Dramens between two sheets of rock. "Rune could open up the earth beneath them," I offered, since it seemed like a simple fix. Rune heard his name and ran over.

"I would have done it by now if it was safe. If I crack the earth too much, she'll splinter beyond my control." His hands touched my dirty skin tenderly . . . so different than the state of the world around us.

"We need those tanks taken care of. My men can handle the animals and find whoever the fuck wields wind and trees! I'm tired of these damn roots and windstorms." My aunt cursed, and I admired her even more.

"The king has the wind. The jackass won't get close to the fight. Sends everyone else to die while he sits in the tree line." Rune pointed his black sword toward two figures sitting casually on their horses. Seeing the sight made me feel better about myself. At least I would be on the battlefield with my warriors when I became Queen.

"We need a miracle." Dris landed and shifted into her armored self.

"I swear they sent all the Dramens in the continent here. They are flooding that portal on the other side of the trees. We are severely outnumbered, and they have three more tanks rolling in. What do you want us to do, Queen Denisiri?" Dris chewed on her lip while her eyes darted around. Rune lifted his blade and stopped a fur-covered Dramen from reaching us. My aunt scanned over her warriors with an assessing gaze.

A thunderous roar echoed across the kingdom. Dramens and Crystorians immediately stopped their battles.

"What was that?" Was this another trick from the Dramens? If they had a secret weapon, we were screwed.

"Up there!" Nyx pointed to the sky.

A black dragon flapped his mighty wings and released a blaze of fire onto the Dramens exiting the portal.

"Is that . . .?" Dris spoke softly. A figure wearing diamond armor sat on top of the black dragon. She had a bow in her hand and fired shots as the dragon neared the ground to douse the Dramens with flames.

"My parents." I smiled and knew the tides of war had turned in our favor.

Chapter Fifty – Three

Rune

I heard the crackling of a portal being created behind us and whirled my sword into it. Lethirya would use this opportunity to attack us. Or maybe Verin himself, if he didn't sip tea with the king of the Dramens while their soldiers fought.

"Nice throw, General." A familiar voice filtered through the portal, and Najen stepped through the blue circle with my sword in his hand. My breaths trembled as more of my soldiers stepped through the portal.

"Queen Desiniri, we have been ordered by Queen Olyndria of Crysia to assist you in battle." Najen bowed and the other men followed, while they watched for attackers. The queen's advisor, Ryka, was the last to walk through the portal and closed it behind her. She also held the power to create portals, and she'd saved our asses because of it.

"General Rune." The queen looked to me and nodded. She left the commanding of my men to me. I barked orders for my beta squad to take down any tanks left. Najen would take the remaining hundred and finish the Dramens.

"Love you." I kissed my woman and ran alongside my warriors with renewed spirit. We were still outnumbered, but my warriors had trained for brute battle like this. While Crystoria's battle strategy was efficient a majority of the time, we'd never faced a Dramen enemy of this size in history to utilize their fighting techniques. Honestly, they were no better than animals with a gun.

A loud roar echoed from our left and Silvio had used his sound wave blasts to knock down twenty Dramens with knives. Sapphira's parents burned countless Dramens while avoiding the areas where golden armor mixed with the enemy. My soldiers moved like a sharp arrow through the Dramen crowd. Even when the coward king through gusts of strong wind toward us, those with shields stepped in the front to direct the air in another direction.

"Dragon!" Dramens screamed around us as Desmire flew directly for the ground. Queen Olyndria jumped off the back of the dragon and landed five feet in front of me. Seconds after her, a large male with light-brown skin and long, black hair landed with a heavy thud. He had swirls of white on his face and down past his black armor. The large male lifted two twin blades. He was Sapphira's father, the dragon shifter with a core of onyx.

"Good work, General Rune." The queen smiled at my shocked expression. She wasn't speaking in riddles anymore. Magic had healed my queen. The only other person who believed in me as much as Sapphira did. She watched me work my way through the ranks and gave me the position of General. She leaped into a group of running

Dramens with her diamond armor glistening, the symbol of Crysia flapping on her cape.

"When this is done, son, you and I are going to have a talk about you being with my daughter," Desmire said.

"Then let's finish this." I lifted my own blade and together we roared at the incoming soldiers, the werewolf and the dragon fighting alongside each other once again. It had to be nice for him to walk on two legs again. I couldn't fathom being stuck inside my werewolf for twenty years.

"Mother!" Sapphira jumped over a broken tank and took down anyone who stood in her way as she hugged her mother.

"I'm so proud of you." Her mother cupped my mate's cheeks and tears rolled down her blood-splattered face. Three fur-covered Dramens raced to the vulnerable moment, and I sunk them into the dirt.

"Father!" Sapphira cried as she saw her dad for the first time as a human in decades. They looked so much alike as he hugged—same skin, upturned eyes, and smile.

"Rune." Sapphira reached out a hand for me as war waged around us. I took her hand and she pulled me into their family embrace. I winced as the hug was uncomfortable for me, but I stayed for my mate. Her father patted me on the back then lunged into battle.

"My warrior," the queen murmured, as she watched every swing of his blade and mighty roar as he took down Dramens in every direction he moved.

"Time to end this, my dear. We will talk soon." The queen hugged her daughter once more and grasped the bow from her shoulder. People dropped as she shot arrow after arrow into the heads of Dramens everywhere. She'd lived for a long time and survived many battles. Queen Olyndria was not a woman to fuck with.

After our forces pushed the remaining Dramens farther into the burning forest, the King blew a horn and all their soldiers retreated. Warriors on our side cheered as the battle had ended. We didn't know if they would regroup or try to fight another day, but for now, we had won. I looked around as warriors in gold and silver embraced each other and thrust their weapons into the air to celebrate. Tor had Nyx lifted into the air with her arms spread wide before she wrapped herself around him for a victory kiss. I scanned the soldiers for more familiar faces and saw a snowy owl fly down, then shift into a flailing Dris. Luckily that damn goat Fae caught her and they embraced each other tightly.

But where was my mate?

I saw her about twenty yards away, near Queen Denisiri. She smiled when our gazes locked and I raced for her.

Suddenly, a crackling portal opened up behind her and I pushed my feet to run faster. Lethirya stepped through and grabbed Sapphira.

"NOO!" I bellowed as I lunged for the portal without fear of where I'd land. If she was being taken somewhere, then I would go with them. The portal closed as I reached it and I landed on the harsh ground.

I roared. In a matter of seconds, Sapphira had been stolen in the victories of our battle. My uncontrolled rage violently shook the earth. My mate, my child, both gone.

"We'll get her back, Rune." Queen Olyndria was there immediately, and I willed myself to remain calm on the outside. I wouldn't hurt my Queen, but I would damn sure hurt someone else right now.

"We'll find her." Nyx stepped into view, as did Tor, Emrys, and Dris, who nodded their agreement to Nyx's words. I wasn't alone this time. I had people who were there for me, who cared, and would help me get Sapphira back.

"We'll get to her, if she doesn't get to us first. Verin won't kill her now. The damage of releasing magic is done. He'll keep her somewhere out of the way or use her as a bargaining tool." Her father stepped up and placed a hand on my shoulder. I didn't know the man and already he acted more like a father than my own. But he had a point. Killing Sapphira wouldn't help Verin in any way. If anything, it would only rally all the kingdoms against him. She was safe for now. My warrior princess would not go quietly, and she'd search for a way to get back to her loved ones. To me. I nodded and took a deep guttural breath.

The victory was short-lived, as we headed back to the palace to strategize. I looked to the rising moon.

"My moon, I will find you." I vowed and the werewolf howled for his mate.

Chapter Fifty – Four

Sapphira

I wrangled free from the tight arms around me as the blinding light of the portal disappeared and landed in the hot sand.

"Hello, little gem."

That eerie voice. I scrambled to my feet. Verin. His daughter walked to his side and stood beside his lithe form. He wore a black tunic with red embroidery and black leather tucked into boots. He looked the same since I last saw him—brown skin with striking golden eyes staring at me.

I looked around, and the evil king laughed.

"My queen thought she was so clever, twisting my mind so I wouldn't search for you," Verin admitted as Lethirya smirked. I held back my rage as I needed to reserve my strength.

"What do you want?" I stood tall in the scorching sun's heat.

"To control the kingdoms, and unite them under my rule." He lifted his hands into the air for emphasis. He took two steps closer and ran his finger down my cheek.

"I need you out of the way," he whispered against me and I jerked away from him. I can't believe I thought this man was my father for most of my life. We were nothing alike.

"While your cohorts stay occupied in finding you, I will be rallying my forces and we will march on Crysia." He strode back to his daughter confidently.

"Hope you live, dear niece. It would be such fun to take the crown from your pretty little head in battle." He chuckled and I lunged for him with my hatchet. Lethirya stepped in front of him and blocked me with her arm and a quick blow to the head.

I fell back into the sand and cursed.

"Goodbye, little gem." Verin looked to his daughter and she twirled her finger into the air. A portal large enough for the both of them opened and I launched to my feet. Lethiyra laughed as I ran for the portal. She and Verin disappeared and the portal vanished. I shifted my head in every direction and saw nothing but mountains of sand.

"Dammit!" I screamed and kicked the stupid sand. One minute I was celebrating the retreat of the Dramens from Fae lands, and the next I was dumped in the desert by my asshole uncle. Rage filled my body as my hatred for Verin marinated in my soul. Apparently, a break was too much to ask before going on another quest to save the world. My mouth had already started to dry, and I had to figure out my next steps. I was in the middle of a desert with no water or knowledge of what desert I stood in.

"Fuck this and fuck you, Verin!" My anger got the better of me as I tried to assess my life. I had nothing that would save me in this situation. No water, no food, nothing. Fire blasted from my hands. I quickly turned that power off. I didn't need more heat.

Shelter. I could do shelter, right? I willed the sand to part and allow the rock to move to the top. The sand swirled and danced in the light breeze but nothing else moved. It was too deep for me to reach with the small amount of earth power I possessed. Even though I knew it to be a pointless act, I tried to form the sand into a shelter. It lasted all of thirty seconds before collapsing back into the desert. I sorted through the powers of everyone I'd touched and tried to think of how they could help me. Verin's poison wouldn't do me much good out here. My mother's speed would help but only for a short while.

I ran down the side of the large sand dune and my foot slipped. Over and over my body tumbled down until I could go no lower. I felt so hopeless, but knew I had to keep trying.

"I'm going to get us out of here, baby," I comforted us both. Anger fueled me to find a way, but the fierce need to survive in order to protect the baby reigned supreme in my head.

"Think, Sapphira, think." I knew I had the power inside me to help, I just had to remember it. A small reprieve of shade had my eyes darting toward the sky.

"Father!" I yelled, hopeful that he flew overhead but when my vision focused on a cloud, I rested back in the sand. Rune and the others would look for me for however long it took. In that time, Verin would be ready to march on Crysia to face off with my mother. I missed them already and wished I could lean on my mate for his never-ending support. He would know what to do . . . how to survive out here.

"Sapphiraaaa." A voice on the wind caught my attention.

"Celestine?" I mumbled and sat up.

"You must rise, my dear. Rise for the world. Rise for your child. Rise for yourself." Celestine's body shimmered five feet away. This time she looked like a ghost. I wondered if we would ever see her again after I burned the Heart Tree.

"I'm lost." Lost not only in the desert but in my mind.

"No, you're not lost, Sapphira. You're afraid."

I remained silent, refusing to say those words aloud. She was right, though. It was so easy for Verin to take me, for the Dramens to overwhelm us in Crystoria, and I wasn't even queen yet. So many people depended on me, even if they didn't know it yet. My hand moved to my stomach, and I wanted to weep for my babe.

"Do you remember what I told you about fear in Crysia?" Celestine floated over to me and kneeled to cover my hand with hers. I didn't answer because I doubted I could resist letting the frustration tears flow if I talked.

"Fear is in your head; the danger is what's real. Fear is your mind telling you to run, and if you run, you'll never know what it's like to live, my dear. To face the danger and leave the fear behind is a true hero's destination." The old seer grinned and patted my hand. I didn't feel it, but I sensed her comfort.

"You took control of your life the day you decided to push past the fear instead of letting it control you. You proved to the world and to yourself that you are a force to be reckoned with—a princess who will become a queen to all. It is time to seize your destiny, Sapphira. You've been preparing for this moment your whole life. Let's make this world right for the baby growing inside you. For all humanity. Rise, Sapphira." Celestine gripped my hand and pulled me up. Slowly, I stood and felt her words weave into my blood.

"You know what to do. Unleash that part of you that has been hidden too long. Become the warrior this world needs you to be."

As she spoke my skin heated, and a familiar power within me stirred. It was new, untouched by my past.

"Thank you," I whispered to the seer, as hope burned in my heart. She was right. I wasn't a damsel in need of saving. I was the master of my life, and it was time to rip the reins back from Destiny's hands. A hint of smoke filled my taste buds, and I let my father's power take over. I assumed I absorbed this side of my father but never had the opportunity to try it, then I forgot about its existence. However, the power was with me all along through my childhood years and had laid dormant through my time as a human.

Pain flared in my back and my bones ached as they grew. I closed my eyes and whimpered from the agony wrecking my body.

"Become the warrior you were always meant to be, Sapphira, and know I will always be there to help you when you need it most."

I opened my eyes and watched the seer disappear. Her job here was done. I took a step and looked down at the massive, blue scaly legs. It worked. Fire blasted from my snout as I roared. The sand shook beneath me as I stretched the massive blue-and-black wings on my back. I could see the clearest details of sand for over a mile and smell the hot air with my new senses. I flapped my wings once, then twice.

"I'm on my way, Rune." I mentally vowed this to the world as well, even though no one could hear me.

I would fly home, even if it took me months to get there. I would bring about a new legacy of peace and unity for humans and Fae alike. And I would finish it by destroying Verin and his reign of darkness with the heart of the dragon beating inside me.

The End . . . For Now . . .

The Final Chase

 I never thought one day I'd make a bet about pedicures to a man and loose.

But of course, I'd never man like him.
Jake Wild. Owner of Wild rescue for exotic animals.
He's everything I'm not, my polar opposite.
I'm heels and my salon,
He's dirt and his creatures.
But much like the animals he cares for, he's got that carnal edge.
He's the type of man you crawl on your hands and knees for.
He bites, he's on the hunt, and now I'm his prey
A chance meeting and a bet started the undeniable attraction between us.
But I'm not giving my heart and soul away that easy, he's going to have to catch me first.
It's the ultimate game of cat and mouse,
But will it be our Final Chase?

Long Drive

There is a long road in everyone's journey in life.
For some people, it's a way to get from one place to another.
For others, it's a search for one's purpose in existence.
For me, the road was where I could find peace.
When everything in my life had shattered, I turned to the road.
And that's where I met him.
Killian Lemarque.
A beautiful truck driver, and my salvation.
One month on the road together is the deal, and when it's over, I will have hopefully figured out what I'm going to do about my torn reality.
But sometimes the road can change everything. Falling in love wasn't part of my plan nor his.

But here we are.
One Month. One Truck. One Long Drive.

How You Get The Girl

As Hollywood's hottest actor, getting a woman in my bed is never a challenge.

But after seeing a feisty woman in bar who was looking for a one-night stand, I knew that her being in my bed wouldn't be enough.

She turned me down, and I thought I'd never see her again.

Fate had other plans though.

Alessandra Rose is now my lead makeup artist for the next four months. Literally, her job is to touch me every day for the duration of filming. Sounds like a win, right?

Nope, she stops me at every hint of a flirt. I'm in uncharted waters for once.

Her argument is good I'll give her that. I'm a good actor, so accepting that it's not all an act would be tough.

But I'm not going anywhere; here heart is my Grammy and him here to win it.

That's how you get the girl.

INSPIRED

Call it pure desperation, or maybe we'd agree it was the lack of sleep that had me signing six weeks of my life away to be bossed around by a life coach. Either way, I was trying to get my life together, and Logan Woodland was going to help.

I thought he'd make me eat healthier, drink more water, and do yoga. What I wasn't expecting, was to be forced to see myself as I was and how far I'd fallen.

But then his program worked.

He'd shown me a life filled with passion and desire. A life where I was stronger and could be the woman I'd never known existed inside me.

I did have a six-week life-changing experience, but now, I wanted more than I'd signed on for.

Him.

Guiding Lights

He sings of suffering. His eyes hold the pain of living in sorrow.
The moment our gaze meets recognition flares within.
We are tortured souls drifting in a sea of darkness.
He knows I have secrets that I'll never tell.
I am numb.
I am broken.
I can never be the guiding light through the darkness he thinks I am.
I have forsaken my past, I rely on keeping myself shut off.
I wish things were different, that maybe we could be each other's lifeline.
But destiny drags us down like an anchor.
He lives his life in the lime light of a famous rock star, and I live in shadows on the run.

I wished I'd known that before I fell for him, but now it's too late.

Blinding Lights

She dances with a passion I'll never know.
Seeing her again tears me at the seams.
She was never mine.
My soul is stained with the darkness of death.
I have killed.
I have tortured.
I have lost.
Her soul is too bright for the shadows I live in
and her determination to be the flame in my heart could
kill us both.
Still, I want her, I crave her.
But not even her blinding lights can fight away the
darkness threatening us both.

But I refuse to lose her, and this time I don't think I can
walk away.

Weighing of the Heart

What happens when the myths of old become reality?

Thalia Alexander has lived her life in peace until her twenty-fifth birthday when she has a strange dream about a man.

A tall, dark, and sexy man that shows up at her work the next morning.

Tristan Jacks is trouble with a capital T, but for some strange reason she is drawn to him like nothing she has ever experienced before. He has this possessiveness and adoration for her that she can't explain. It's like they have known each other forever.

Thalia's strange dreams continue to stalk her as her relationship with Tristan builds to be a love that will last the ages.

And when those dreams and reality start to clash, will Thalia be able to handle the truth?

Could the world of ancient myths truly exist in modern times?

Evergreen

It was supposed to be an easy stakeout.
Until a bunch of bachelorettes mobbed me, changing my life forever.

I couldn't get Andi Slaton, with her red hair, blue eyes, and cotton candy-flavored lip gloss, out of my head.

But when she offers herself to aid the FBI to help me take down the biggest criminal family in Tampa, Florida, my very sanity is put to the test watching her spend time with my arch enemy.

She's everything I want, I will be everything to her.
We will be Evergreen.

Acknowledgments

After writing so many books, you think this section would be easier. Lol I'm just so beyond grateful for anyone who breaths in the direction of my books let alone buys it and gives it a shot. So dearest readers, bloggers, bookstagrammers, everyone... I appreciate you more than words can express. Thank you from the very depths of my being.

I appreciate all the support that's been given to from my friends, my alpha/beta readers, Sarah for getting me in last minute for the cover, Lorraine for her amazing editing skills, and Virginia for proofing this story like a boss. Thank you to my Fairies, the best group ever.

My husband and kiddo have been then best. This pandemic changed so much for us, and being home to write has literally been a dream come true. Thank you fam.

Thank you. I literally could not do any of this without every single one of your support. I'm the luckiest author in the world

About the Author

Jessica Florence writes the stories that her fellow nerds yearn for.

From Superheroes to Sexy Truckers, Jessica is known to give readers unique tales of hope where love conquers all. Stories that melt away reality and take you on a journey with the characters. If escapism is what you are looking for, then look no further. Jessica is the Queen of weaving the tales you may not normally pick up but find yourself not being able to put down.

Jessica's always had a love of reading, and her love of books lead her to start writing in the 9th grade. She quickly learned that storytelling was her passion. Inspired by movies, music, and her personal life she writes like it's the very air she breathes. Through her writing it's evident that she lives for the stories she creates.

Jessica grew up in North Carolina, and currently resides in Southwest Florida with her daughter, husband, and German Shepherd. She loves to be outside, write in her hammock, and collect tea mugs.

CONNECT WITH J-FLO:

→ FACEBOOK: facebook.com/jessicaflorenceauthor
→ INSTAGRAM: Instagram.com/authorjessicaflorence
→ TWITTER: twitter.com/@Florence_jess
→ PINTEREST: pinterest.com/florencejess
→ WEBSITE: www.Jessicaflorenceauthor.com

Made in the USA
Monee, IL
03 January 2021

56360359R00173